Ain't It Just Like a Human?

Written by Dan White

Based on the memories of Kevin O'Connor

Introduction

This book is about the life and times of Kevin O'Connor. Kevin was born in 1943 and was seventy-six years old when the book was researched and written in early 2020. He stands six-foot tall with a typical paunch for an older man and has striking, curly, silvery-white hair.

Kevin was born and spent much of his childhood in Dublin before moving over to England in 1956. I met Kevin and his wife Kathleen in May 2018 having responded to a post on a local community web forum asking for a volunteer to help an elderly couple learn how to use their new android tablet. Sadly, after thirty years together, Kevin and Kathleen split up soon after I met them, but I remained in contact with Kevin and got to know him well over the coming months. As Kevin told me many stories about his turbulent life and strained family relationships, I began to think that his story would be worth recording. Kevin has led a life that is remarkable in many ways. He has travelled across most of Europe, been accused of child-abduction and domestic abuse and has appeared at the European Court of Human Rights in Strasbourg. Kevin was also keen for me to write the book, so we met during the first three months of 2020 for a series of interviews.

We met in the sitting room of Kevin's modest council bungalow in Wellesbourne, Warwickshire. The room has a large window, but Kevin prefers to keep the curtains partially drawn, but not so much as to damage the amaryllis that sits on the windowsill - a moving in present from a friend from church. Below the window is a small wooden dining table and three chairs. Vinegar, salt and a bottle of brown sauce are permanently on the table which is where Kevin eats all his meals. The floor is covered in linoleum which extends to all the other rooms. The room is sparsely decorated but it has a stark oil painting hanging over an electric fireplace that is entirely decorative. It doesn't produce any heat, but it looks like a coal fire and gives the room some much needed character. There are a couple of family photos and a few postcards on the mantelpiece above. We sit in armchairs facing the fireplace as we talk, usually holding cups of tea. There are piles of papers and envelopes beneath and behind a small coffee table next to Kevin, upon which he keeps his mobile phone and a pocket diary. Kevin has repurposed the diary as a notepad where he keeps important names, phone numbers and appointment details. Kevin is usually wearing a white vest with holes in it and a pair of draw-string boxer shorts. We tend to talk for two or three hours with a break for more tea and a biscuit or cake. This book is an account of Kevin's life based entirely on his memories. The story is presented in the form of dialogue, but it is far from being a direct transcript of the interviews. The descriptions of the dramatic and sometimes shocking events in Kevin's life all follow his recollections accurately but they were retold in a very fragmented and non-chronological fashion, as you might expect. Also, a few of the names and incidental details have been changed. I believe that Kevin's account is candid, but I sensed that, like any of us would do when quizzed about every moment of our life, Kevin is holding back a few details in places, as is his prerogative.

Incidentally, the book title comes from the song 'Here Comes That Rainbow Again' originally sung by Kris

Kristofferson but later adopted by Johnny Cash, one of Kevin's favourite artists. The lyrics are based on a heart-warming episode from John Steinbeck's novel 'The Grapes of Wrath.' They describe a small act of kindness by a waitress to two 'Okie' kids (from poor Oklahoman farming families) that symbolises how the goodness of humanity can find its way to the surface, despite disappointment and hardship. This is just like Kevin.

Chapter 1

Dublin

Hi Kevin. It's good you see you again.
Hello young man! Come in, come in. Let me take your coat.

It's freezing out there.
I know. I've put the heating up on so it should be nice and warm. Cup of tea?

Yes please.
Come through to the kitchen. The kettle's already boiled. Hang on a sec - it won't take long. Do you take sugar?

Just one, thanks.
OK, here you go.

What are you using there?
Oh this? This is good stuff. It's organic. You use it instead of sugar.

Let's take a look. Oh - it's agave.
It's natural. Nothing added at all.

Do you buy a lot of organic products?
Oh yes. They're better for you, you know? No chemicals either.

When did you start buying organic?
A long time ago. If I could afford it. I worked on a farm when I was a boy, a young man. This was a long time ago - I was only fifteen. And I saw what they were putting on the land and it frightened the life out of me. But with organic, you're limiting the chemicals in your body, you know? It was an eye opener when I worked on that farm.

What do you mean?
It was these crystals and things they were using. The thought of that going on the land. And, of course, it transfers to the rivers. And they're growing the grass with that and the cows come and eat the grass and it goes into the milk, and it goes into the meat et cetera, et cetera. I thought, that can't be healthy, you know? That's when I started buying organic, but it was expensive back then. I mean really expensive. It would cost you a few pound for a few eggs - and that's when a few pound was a lot, you know? And I didn't have much money back then so I couldn't always afford it. It's so cheap now. There's almost no difference in price. These are organic, these yoghurts, see? Marks & Spencer's.

You shop at Marks & Spencer's?
Yes, because they have the best organic.

Maybe I'll give organic a try.
You won't regret it!

So, are you ready to start this book we've been talking about?
Oh yes. I've been looking forward to it.

Great. Are you OK if I start recording?
Yes, of course.

Obviously, I know you already, but for the recording: what is your name?
My first name is Ronald and my second name is Kevin and my surname: O'Connor. Ronald Kevin O'Connor. My mum called me Ronald after a sea captain that was one of her relations and he was called Ronald. Dad went ballistic, virtually, because he said it was too posh, too English! He was very 'Irish, Irish' if you know what I mean? But she stuck to her guns and she still called me Ronald.

Where were you born?
I was born in Dublin in October 1943. The war had just about ended then. We lived on North Circular Road. Number four, I think it was. I lived with my Dad. John Joseph O'Connor he was called. And my mum, and my sisters and my two brothers as well.

What was your mum's name?
My mum was called Edith O'Connor, but she was called Edith Hewitt before she got married.

What were your siblings called?
There was Norman, he's the oldest and then there was my brother Jackie and I'm the youngest of the boys. I have three sisters altogether: Marie, then Patricia - older than me - and Phyllis, she was the youngest.

What was your house like?
A lovely house we had. Opposite us was St. Peter's Church. It was just across the road. We had a big house. Four or five bedrooms. Big rooms too. I had to share with my sisters. They would have one double bed for the three of them and I had a single bed, over by the wall. We were in together because we had other people living there as well.

8

Who else lived in the house?
One of my uncles had one of the rooms for his
dentist's practice. That was on the ground level at the very
front of the house with the windows that curve out - I don't
know what you call them.

Bay windows?
I think so, yes. They're curved to make the room bigger. I
didn't go to the dentist, but he was there, so it was handy if
you wanted to.

Tell me about your part of the house.
The kitchen was lovely. I can still see it now - all red tiles.
Beautiful it was. I was getting these terrible migraines then.
My mum used to use something called Cardinal polish to
keep the tiles looking lovely, but the trouble is, it gave off
something.

What do you mean?
It gave off a smell. An odour. I said, 'Please mum, don't
use that!' But she said, 'I've got to, it's the only way to
keep it all looking nice.' About once a week she did that but
of course I'd get really sick because I was affected by the
migraine and the smell from the Cardinal polish. It was a
big kitchen. It had a big, solid table. On the left-hand side
was the fireplace and a stove above the fireplace. Every so
many weeks she used to blacken it.

Blacken it?
Yeah, you know, she'd use this black stuff to keep it
looking nice. Not a paint. It was like a paste. It was all
clean after you wiped it off.

Did you spend much time in the kitchen?
I did. My mum was always there, you see, and I used to
help her. She was always making cakes or biscuits or

9

something. We had these big mixing bowls and she'd be mixing something, and she'd say, 'Can you take over, Ronnie?' And I'd say, 'Yeah, of course,' and I'd carry on mixing the stuff while she was doing something else. You had to keep mixing it otherwise it would go funny. Without knowing, I was learning how to cook. That's how I got to work in kitchens, in hotels and all that, when I was older.

Speaking of kitchens, is that tea ready?
Yes, I think it should be ready by now. I'll go and fetch it... Here you go. Mind not to spill it.

What kinds of food did your mum prepare for you all?
Every Sunday, we'd have a fantastic lunch. Usually, some sort of beef. I don't remember us having chicken or pork or anything - it was mostly beef. Some potatoes with it - roasters and all that. I'd help her peel the potatoes and things because there were a lot of us, you know? And mammy used to do this beautiful cake - a big fruitcake. We always had that. It was terrific.

Was your mum a good cook?
Not to start with. Apparently, when she got together first with my dad, she couldn't cook at all. She told me about when they had their first turkey for Christmas. They didn't do like they do now. You had to take all the things out, the giblets and all. But she didn't know about that, so she didn't. Consequently, of course, it stank the place out and we couldn't eat it. My dad was the one knew how to cook so he taught her, and she picked everything up quick so after that, she was a fantastic cook. He didn't do any cooking, but he knew how to do things and he told her how to do it.

What would you eat on special occasions?
Like Christmas, do you mean?

Yes.

Well, we were very lucky because every year, our uncle used to enter for this thing and some of the prizes was turkeys. And every year, without fail, he used to win! About two or three turkeys he used to win, every year. Thinking back, it may have been fixed but I don't know. And he'd give us one, of course. My mum had learnt to cook by then, so we had a real feast. A beautiful, big turkey and all the trimmings - the veg and everything like that. She used to do a lovely spread for Christmas. We'd all sit around this massive table. We'd tuck into the turkey and, after that, the Christmas pudding. Mum did Christmas puddings using the cloth, you know, which is the nicest way. Muslim, I think it's called - she did them in that. We were well fed, that's for sure!

So, Christmas was important to the family.

Yes, of course! We all celebrated Christmas, being Catholic and all. An important time, you know? We had early mass, about eleven or twelve at night. It was only across the road from us as I said.

Who went to early mass from your family?

They didn't all go - it was their choice, you know? I used to go, obviously, because I was in the choir because I had a good voice, even back then. And probably my dad would go. My mum didn't go. Just me and my dad, really.

Did you give presents to one another?

Not really, no. We didn't have much money. Just very simple things, you know, and maybe a stocking.

What would be in the stocking?

Fruit, mostly. Oranges and apples and things like that. Nothing like the kids nowadays get. Phyllis usually got something quite good. I remember a little pram or something. I do remember getting a fort, like they had in the Americas. Only a little one. A cowboy fort thing and little soldiers, lead soldiers - they're not allowed now. If I'd have kept them, they'd have been valuable now, wouldn't they? I'd play with that on my own - Phyllis wasn't interested, obviously, in soldiers and that. It didn't take much to entertain me, you know?

Do any other presents stick in your mind?
One of the best Christmases I do remember, my dad brought this car in. Obviously, it was second hand and he had it painted red. I knew it had been painted because it was still wet! Well at least he did something, my dad, which was unusual for him. This car was amazing to me. I can still see it now. It was like, what do you call it? Not a car, a bit like a truck, for going in fields, over land?

A Land Rover?
A Jeep! It was an impression on a Jeep, and I was over the moon when I saw it. I couldn't wait to get out in the garden with it and everything. No motors - just pedals. I'd go all around the garden with it and down the lane. I showed it off to the other kids and they said, 'Ooh that's good!"

How did you celebrate birthdays?
I remember Phyllis's birthdays. People came round and lots of food - a party and all. My mum used to make a fuss of her, but she wouldn't do it for me. I said, 'Why is that?' And she said, 'Well it's because she's a girl - boys don't need things like that.' That was her excuse. I don't know where she got that idea from. I felt a bit left out because when she's having her birthday, mum would make a nice cake for her and some little cakes as well and get a few people around. Made a real effort. For some reason she wouldn't do that for me. It was because she was the youngest, I suppose. I maybe got a card or something. My mum never did cakes for me.

What else do you recall about the house?
I remember there was one part, when you went up by the stairs, in the hall, like - for some reason it always got really cold there. The temperature suddenly dropped, and you could see your breath. Just in that one spot there. We always said it was a bit haunted or there had been something funny going on there. You could always notice it when you went through there. It gave you the willies!

Did you have a living room?
The living room went off the kitchen. We used to spend a bit of time in there, I 'spose. We listened to the radio a lot. The Archers - la, la la, la la, lar lar, la, la la, la lar lar. And Life with the Lyons. That was an American family who came over to England and it was about their adventures and that. Bebe Daniels and Ben Lyon - that was the husband and wife. Just what they were getting up to, their life and all, and they introduced us to their daughter and the rest of the family. They were real people. It was really fantastic. We never used to miss that. And my mum used to listen to it in the kitchen, while we were cooking. The radio was really great - such company, you know? Such comfort.

Did you listen to music?
Oh yes. It wasn't the sixties yet, so it was easy listening sort of stuff - no rock and roll! It hadn't really started, all this pop stuff. Just the old singers like Frankie Vaughan and people like that. And Frankie Laine. He brought that one out and made a big hit out of it 'I Believe'. Some of them were religious and some of them weren't. Lovely music.

Apart from the dentist downstairs, did anyone else live in the house?
We had a gentleman living with us, who was an uncle. Charlie he was called. He was lovely, he was. He had his own room and often I'd go up to the room and he'd tell me about things that happened during the war. About how they

13

fought during the war. He was in the second world war, obviously. It was interesting to hear. I was only a kid at the time. He was related to us somewhere along the line, on my mother's side, as far as I can make out. He had his own room in our house. He was a lovely old boy. He didn't get on with my dad. He tried, I 'spose, to avoid my dad as much as possible but it's not easy when you're in the same house. What he thought about what was going on, what my dad was doing and all, I don't know. He was getting on a bit. He eventually joined the ones in London - the ex-service people in London? Loved it there, he did.

The Chelsea Pensioners?
Yeah - the Chelsea Pensioners! He went and joined them. He thought, well, he probably got fed up with my dad, being like he was and everything. You know, he obviously didn't agree with what was going on. He was a real sweet man.

What do you mean he didn't agree with what was going on?
Well, my dad wasn't the best, to put it mildly. He was very good with his fists, shall we say.

He hit you?
Oh yes. All the time. He hit all the boys.

Did he hit the girls?
No, he wouldn't hit the girls. We found out later that he was interfering with the girls. Sexually I mean. But he never hit them. And I think my mum just turned a blind eye to it because she didn't want to keep having to get pregnant, having babies all the time. So she, in a way, was bad - but she tried. She obviously didn't want to confront him, you know?

Was she scared?
I think so, yes.

14

Did he ever touch you?
Yes, he hit me all the time.

No, I mean… sexually?
Ah, well, no. He made a fatal mistake, you see, when I was five. I came in and I'd got these new shorts on, which was rare. They were a treat my mum had bought me. And I went in to show them and he put his hand up my leg and I told my mum and she went ballistic. I mean ballistic! She put up a knife to his throat. I can still see it now. 'You ever touch him again,' she said, 'and I'll kill you,' she said. And she would have too. After that he never bothered with me again.

Wow.
I know. If he was alive today, he'd be on the sex offenders register - no question about it at all. Also, too, he was very violent. With all of us. Knocking us about, you know? And he had a big ring, a big old ring, and when he hit you, of course, you'd end up with the impression of the ring on the side of your face. He never showed any affection at all. He was cold as ice.

I'm sorry.
Don't worry, it was a long time ago. And mammy was there. She was the one that we got the love from, the affection.

Chapter 2

Kevin's Dad

Was your dad violent outside the family?
Oh yes. He was a nasty man. Violent with everyone, he
was. I remember one time, there was this chap that got
funny with me for some reason. Just in the street. In
Arndale Avenue, in Dublin. I don't know what it was, but I
went back and told my dad. I mentioned to my dad that he
was threatening me, this bloke, and he said, 'What was he
like?' So, I told him.

What happened?
Well, my dad went and saw him and sorted him out. He
gave him a right beating, didn't he? A right pasting.

Was the man injured?
Of course he was. He was hospitalized!

How often was he violent with you and your brothers?
Well, you know, how many eggs are in a basket? How long
is a piece of string, you know? It's very hard to say. We all
got hurt loads of times - they all blur into one. It was
regular; it was the usual thing, that's all. And so violent, you
know? We were all scared of him, that's for sure. In the
evening, we used to dread him coming home, you know?

Because we knew what it meant. Proper fear, it was, because he was so strong. And so mean to us.

Do any particular incidents stick in your mind?
I remember Norman, that's my oldest brother - he's gone a few years now - I remember him being thrown from one room to another by my dad and hitting the wall. I remember him going down the wall with blood all the way down, on the wallpaper. That's no exaggeration.

That memory must have affected you.
It did! I remember when Norman slipped down the wall, there was blood everywhere. I wasn't surprised - it was nothing unusual - but I was still shocked, you know? That was nearly seventy years ago but it I can still see it now. My dad wasn't built like me, but he was so strong.

Was your dad a drinking man?
You could say! He was very fond of the booze. He was in the pub most days, drinking our money away.

Is that what made him violent?
Not really, no. It wasn't only if he came in drunk - which he did, a lot - it was just the same when he was sober.

Did you ever stand up to your dad?
No, never. I was too young, really. He was too strong. I mean he was really strong, even though he was only thin, you know? Apparently, he was in the pub one day, and a bouncer, built like a juggernaut - he said something my dad didn't like, and my dad grabbed him and lifted him off his feet and threw him out the window. That's how strong he was, and I was only little. I was under five foot when I was seventeen, before I shot up.

Did he ever hit your mum?
I honestly don't know. I don't think so - not exactly. My

mum stood in front of us many times, to try and stop us getting a beating and, of course, she got hit - you know, trying to protect us. But he never hit women, not on purpose anyway. Also, my mum's mum, she had him made up, she couldn't stand him, and she tried to protect us. She made me laugh, she was only little! She was Jewish, by the way - so I've got Jewish blood in me.

Doesn't that make you Jewish?
What do you mean?

If your mum's mum was Jewish, so was your mum and so are you!
Don't be daft, I'm a Catholic!

If you say so.
Well I was born Catholic, but that's another story. If I was Jewish, I'd be saying 'I've got to pick a pocket or two, boys, I've got to pick a pocket or two!'

Is that your Jewish accent?
Yeah… ha… ha…ha! I'm only kidding.

Is that from 'Oliver'?
Yes. It has some great songs.

Are you OK talking about your dad and how violent he was?
I'm too old to worry about that. What's done is done, that's what I say.

OK. So, can you remember any other specific times when your dad was violent?
There was one time I remember because my sister Patricia reminded me of something when I was talking to her a few weeks ago. This one time, Patricia came in and I wasn't very well. I was in bed ill with something or other - I don't

18

know what it was. And he was laying into me.

He hit you when you were ill?
Yes, I'm afraid so. I was only about five or six. Patricia said, 'Leave him alone!' But he wouldn't take any notice. He said, 'You keep out of it!' She said, 'If you don't leave him alone,' she said, 'I'm going to get the police.' That was my sister. Always looking out for me.

What did she do?
She didn't get the police, but instead she did go and call the doctor - our local doctor. And he came in and he saw the mess I was in. My dad had been laying into me, so I wasn't very well. I was already ill and he'd thumped me a few times. And he said, the doctor said, 'If you don't stop that now, I'm gonna phone the police - leave that boy alone!' And that stopped him.

Why didn't the doctor phone the police?
Well that's now - nowadays they would. They threatened, in my day. 'If you don't leave him alone, we'll do something'. But, obviously, the doctor was not very impressed, you know? But that's what it was like, as I said, with the boys. He never touched the girls. Well, he never touched the girls with the fists, if you know what I mean? But he touched the girls in other ways. And, um, obviously that's affected them, I suppose. Bound to of. But that's what it was like. I mean it was a lovely house but, you know?

Did he ever hit you in public?
Oh no. Always in the house - behind closed doors. People never knew what he was like. They'd go to church and they'd think, what a lovely man! They didn't know what he was like, did they?

How did your parents get together?
They played tennis, table tennis. He won some sort of

awards, some medals for it. That's what brought them together. He was very handsome. All the women were after him in the tennis club. She thought she'd done really well getting him, you know? I saw some photos of him when he was young. He was so handsome. He looked like what's his name, that actor? Errol Flynn. He looked a bit like him. All the women were mad about him, but they didn't live with him, did they? Biggest mistake she ever made in her life.

What else do you remember about your dad?
Well, he was one of the lieutenants in the IRA, believe it or not.

Really?
He was, yeah. Of course, the IRA were justified because they were fighting for their country. He told me the British had let these people out of prison, murderers they were. The Black and Tans they were called. They were sent over by the British. Out and out murderers. They were given a choice: either get hung or go over to Ireland. So, they went over to Ireland and they went shooting. They shot babies in their prams! Terrible things. And that's how the IRA was formed. That's what started it all because they thought, well, we're not going to just sit there, you know, and let you come and murder our people and everything. A bit like the French resistance, shall we say? You know - they'd blow up places and things. They'd fight, which you can't blame them.

You said your father was a lieutenant?
Yeah. He was very pro-Irish. One of the lieutenants, he was, in his twenties. He told us about it, said things he'd done and all, so I know it was true. He said what had happened and how they used to fight for their country, but he didn't go into too much detail about it.It's history, you know? That's how the real IRA started, not the ones now. They had a right to do what they did. 1916 is when it all

came to a head when the IRA were really starting to fight this lot, you know, the English. But it cost a lot of lives, too.

I remember the bombings in the and eighties and nineties. They were bad times.

Speaking of bad times, do you remember any good times with your father?
There were some good moments; it wasn't all bad. I remember we all enjoyed music together, including my dad. He taught himself how to play the piano, the fiddle and the harmonica. Really well, I mean. Self-taught completely. He used to play everywhere. Different places - pubs and things. To entertain. Through that, of course, I inherited the thing for music. I've got a good ear for it, put it that way. I got that from him, I think. Like, for example, I hear something, I only have to hear it a few times, and it's there. I mean I can still remember songs that I heard when I was little. He'd often play music at home. He used to take the harmonica up, or the fiddle, and play for a while. And I would sing. I mean even my dad, he knew I was able to sing. He wanted me to get on this radio show 'cos he knew the bloke that ran it. It was like Opportunity Knocks, that type of thing.

> Oh, the school around the corner's just the same
> The school that taught you how to play the game
> It hasn't changed at all
> The old tables in the hall
> Oh, the school around the corner's just the same

That's how they used to introduce the show. That's how they used to start with the music and then they'd come on, these acts - kids and all, you know? 'I've got a son,' he said, 'and he's got a terrific voice.' So, you see, he did realise that. 'You should have him on your show,' he said.

But it was too late. He'd missed the chance. He wasn't happy about that, I can tell you.

Do you have any other fond memories of your dad?
When he got ill, really ill, of course, I had to help him. This was much later, of course. For example, we had an immersion put in and it meant getting this thing into the tank. Really difficult it was, and he couldn't do it because it was starting to tell on him, the illness, so I helped him do it. But we didn't have a lot together. A shame, really. Could have been nice. That's why I'm so devastated losing my own sons.

Chapter 3

Kevin's Mum

What was your mother like?
My mum, she was a lovely, absolutely lovely. When I was five, I had meningitis, which is deadly, and my mum got me over that. But then I discovered later than my mum had healing. I mean she was like a healer. And she passed that on to me because later on, when I lived in Cheltenham, this is quite a while later, I helped people to heal, you know? And I think that came from her because she got me over meningitis. She was lovely, my mum - too good for him. Far too good for him.

What do you remember most about your mum?
She used to sing. I remember her always singing. I learnt a load of songs listening to her. She had nothing to sing about, but she sang anyway. It kept her going, I suppose. She's who I got the voice from. She knew loads of songs. I listened to them and without knowing it, I was recording them in my head.

Which songs did your mum sing?
She sang so many songs. She was singing all the time! One of her favourite songs, 'Mr. Wonderful, That's You' it's called. She used to sing it a lot.

Have you always enjoyed singing?
Oh, yeah! When I was seven, I remember, a film came out
with Norman Wisdom, right? And in it he wrote this song
called, er, 'Don't Laugh At Me 'cause I'm a Fool'. You
probably wouldn't of heard of it - before your time. That
was one he brought out. And I thought, I know what I'm
going to do. There was a talent contest in my school. I was
only seven. I'm gonna go as Norman Wisdom. So, I got this
little jacket that was too small because that's the way he
used to dress. And a little cap thing, you know? And I went
on and I won it. I actually won it!

How did you learn the song?
I listened to it, to him singing it. I got the record, that's all.
Somebody bought the record I 'spose - my mum probably.
And he actually wrote that himself, for the film. And
funnily enough, on Facebook a few weeks ago it showed
him singing on there.

Really?
Yeah! And I thought - memories, you know? It brings back
so many memories! I was seven and I can still remember all
the words, you see?

What other singing do you remember?
Well, right across from us was the church, the main church:
St. Peter's. My father used to go there quite regular and,
course, I was in with the choir over there. It was a big choir
as well. Sometimes I used to do a solo - singing on my own,
you know - which was an honour, really. The choirmaster,
he was a lovely man, he always said to me, 'When your
voice breaks, you're going to go into opera,' he said. 'With
your voice you'll do really well,' he said. Trouble is when it
started breaking, it went lower and lower and lower. I
thought, well, what am I going to do? I can't do opera -
that's no good for opera. I thought, hmmm - what about

24

country? I listened to it a lot. Sometimes on the radio but also playing records and things. My favourite of all was Jim Reeves. He was my idol when I was growing up. He did all these songs and they were all so lovely. I remember this one called 'I Love You Because':

Did your mum go to church?
Not always. There was a bit of a conflict, you see, because my mum, originally, when she married my dad, she was a Protestant. And she had to change her religion to marry him, because that's the way they work, in the church. But she never really became a proper Catholic, you know what I mean? Not deep down inside, she didn't. Not in her heart. But my dad was quite religious, in a way, I suppose.

Did you mum work?
My mum was mostly doing housework, really. She did a little bit, I remember, of as you'd call nursing. Just in the hospital. What do you call it? Auxiliary nursing. Not the top nurses, just auxiliary they call them. But she was very good at that. Just like her mum.

Tell me about your mum's mum.
She was so lovely. She used to come to our house every so often and, of course, she absolutely hated my dad! Hated him. She said to my mum, 'You should never have got in with him!' And she was right, of course. Anyway, you've got to laugh - she was only a little woman - she stood up to my dad. One time, she tried to pick a chair up and hit him over the head! And of course, he just took it off her. And she picked up something else and he just took it off her again! It was like a comedy. A bloody carry on! But she tried, bless her.

Did your mum have any brothers or sisters?
I don't remember her having any, no. She might have had but I don't think she did, actually. She might have been an

25

only child. But there was other relations my mum was very fond of. There was one, Aunty Rita we called her, and as far as I know she's still alive. She was really nice - a generous person, you know? She'd come over and spend time with us. She had no time for my dad, because she knew what he was like, of course - how violent he was and all, and all the drinking as well.

Did she visit you often?
She used to come around a fair amount - not that much - but we always used to look forward to her coming because she used to have something with her - a little present or something like that. She was really lovely. And my mum and her were really good friends, whenever they were together. I don't know if they went to school together, but they knew each other really well.

Did you know your mum's dad?
No, I never met him. Sadly my mum's dad and my dad's dad were both gone before I was born, although I sometimes heard a bit about him.

How did your mum's mum get on with you and your siblings?
She was a great one for boys. She loved boys, not girls so much. She said girls were all cats. So, every so often, she used to have us over in Bray where she lived. She had a little bungalow at a seaside place. And we'd go over there and that was away from my dad - an escape. I remember how people were, when they saw me there. I had curly hair, so people used to run their hands in my hair like that because of the curls, you know? Ooh he's got lovely hair, they'd say. I thought, I wish they'd stop - get off! Buy it was nice, really. They meant well, you know? She was very proud of us and all. We had this double bed, which I shared with her. I remember one night, well, I had to go away right, to use the pot. A little pot which we used to use.

26

That's the way they were then. And she was out cold. Anyway, I was on the pot and I come back, and she thought I was a bloody ghost coming up! In fact, it was only me. And we laughed! She was lovely. A lovely, lovely lady.

What did you do at the seaside?
Oh, you know, we'd go around, have a look at the things and buy some of the rock, and things like that? She spoilt us. Only the boys. She didn't bother with my sisters at all. It was mostly me because I was the youngest. Jackie was in his twenties by then.

Did you know your dad's mum?
Yes, I did. She was a big lady. About six foot and she weighed over thirty stone. Big, big lady! She had this beautiful hair. Long, silver hair right down to her bum. It was like a rope. I can picture her now, brushing it. Ah, she was lovely. I was only five or six when she died which is a shame really, but I got to know her. She ruled the roost, you know? She had the boys, at least four or five of them - a whole load of sons, and the husband was only a little guy. Obviously, she was the boss, you know? She wasn't strict with us, but she was with my dad. She had to be with all those sons. I used to go to her little house every so often, during the week sometime. We'd go there straight from school; her house wasn't that far from the school. And she'd spoil us, make a fuss of us with home-made bread that she'd do and little treats. I was quite upset when she died but she was in her nineties. They said she died of a fatty heart, but who would care if you're ninety-eight!

Do you remember any of your dad's brothers?
I met a few of them but most of them didn't make an impression on me, put it like that. The one that sticks in my mind is the one that was in partnership with my dad. Alfie, I think he was called. A nice bloke. He always had sweets for us - we were only little - you know what kids are like.

He always brought some sort of sweets, what do you call them? At that time, I remember there was this thing on the radio… Spangles they were called. They were Hop-along-Cassidy's favourite sweets! That's going back a long time. Anyway, he'd bring them as a treat for us, in his pocket. What have I got here? You know, teasing us like that. Nice teasing. And of course, we'd be all: woowoooo! - so excited! And also too, he was generous at Christmas. He didn't usually come over for Christmas, but he'd always bring a turkey over. I don't know how he managed it - whether he fiddled it I don't know. Maybe he did? He used to win this thing every year. Of course, I didn't think about it at the time, you know, whether it was suspicious or not.

Tell me about your brothers.
Norman, the oldest, he was into electronics. He was a very clever man, but he also had a good voice which he never bothered using. Then there was my brother Jackie, the entertainer one who worked at Pontins and then ended up in Australia.

What about your sisters?
My oldest sister, Marie - she's the sister from hell. She's got a lot of my dad in her I'm afraid. A hell of a lot of him in her. We never got on. I didn't have much to do with her when I was little.

What about Patricia?
We always got on well, her and me. We were really close, you know? We still are. She sent me this lovely Aran sweater for my birthday - my last birthday. She always looked after me. And she was very good looking. I'm not kidding - she was absolutely stunning in looks.

And Phyllis?
She was a bit spoilt, I think. Because Phyllis was the last out - I mean the last to come along - our mum seemed to do

things for her more than she did for me and the others. She was a lovely looking little thing, but she was just a bit spoilt. She was the youngest so you can't blame my mum, really.

Chapter 4

The Neighbourhood

Where did you go to school?
I went to St. Peter's school. Just an ordinary school. The teachers were horrible. They were sadists really, to put it mildly. I'm not exaggerating. They wouldn't get away with what they did then. They should have run a concentration camp really. They were better suited to that job, that's for sure!

Were you good at schoolwork?
I was way ahead of myself with the English because my sister Trisha - she's four years older than me - she took me under her wing. We got on like that. More than the other sisters. It's just the way we were. Very close. We still are. And she took the trouble to teach me how to read. So, I was reading newspapers at five. And by the time I went to school, of course, I was ahead of all the other kids, weren't I? With the reading. My English was top. But Maths: I'm absolute rubbish! And if you were like that about anything, this teacher, I still remember his name, Mr. Nevin, he'd have it in for you. Only a short-arsed little bloke he was but he was a sadist.

What did he do?

His favourite was… he had a dog's collar, right, which he put around your neck and you went down on all fours and he kicked you around the classroom to the laughter of all the other kids.

Really?
Oh, yeah. I told you: sadists, they were. And this was the fifties - they could get away with anything then. Mr Nevin was the worst. I was bad at maths. If you were bad at a thing, he'd make a fool of you.

Do you remember any other teachers?
There was the head teacher called Mr. Walsh. He, apparently, was dying of slow cancer. Took years to kill him. And because he was suffering, the poor man - he was obviously in pain - he took it out on the kids, I'm afraid. He used to belt the hell out of us with this leather strap thing. He had it made special. Just over a foot long. In it was coins, you know, the old-fashioned pennies?

Like 2p coins?
Yes, but a bit bigger than that. It had a proper handle, a wooden handle. Inside the strap was pennies. All these pennies were stitched into it. About twelve I 'spose. If you were late, just a few minutes late, he would stick to us for that. You're gonna see Mr. Walsh. You're gonna see Mr. Walsh; You're gonna see Mr. Walsh. We'd all be in a queue. Oh, god no! we'd say. Being told you're in the queue, that was like someone saying to you you're going to the gallows 'cos we knew what we were all going to get. Always six on the hands. Six of the best, they call it. Believe me, you didn't know what hit you, after. You could always tell the kids that had been to see Mr. Walsh because they come out with their hands under their arms. The pain doesn't go in your hand, it goes under your arms. That's where the pain goes. It travels, I suppose, up your arm. The poor man was probably in a lot of pain. He took it out

without meaning to, I suppose, on the kids. I don't think he ever had kids of his own. Of course, you couldn't get away from it, because there was no good complaining to my father 'cos he used to knock it out all of us anyway.

Were all your teachers cruel?
There was one teacher, Mr O'Neal, and he was lovely. Totally different to the others, a totally different person altogether. You could talk to him and he was very understanding. He didn't believe in what the others were doing.

What do you remember about your neighbours?
I remember a family called the Daley's. I felt really sorry for them. She had about twenty-five kids. Her husband was a drunk and all the money, of course, went on the booze. I can still see them now in the middle of winter. We used to get bad winters, really bad winters, I mean. I see them now, the Daley's, the boys, come there with their little pumps, just white little pumps in the middle of winter. And their noses, of course, all runny, you know, 'cos they had this constant cold? And little jackets on, not dressed the way you should be. Like a T-shirt type thing: no good in temperatures like that. Because she couldn't afford to dress them. He was drinking all the money.

Did your family have more money than most?
We didn't have a lot of money, but we had more than most, I 'spose, because my dad had a good job. He had a partnership, he and his brother, as I was telling you. They were in charge of Interphones. They used to do all the, what do you call it? They had all these operators, all in line, they'd put you through to different numbers...

Switchboards?
Yeah, switchboards, that's it. My dad and his brother - that was their job. They made all these. They actually made

them - designed them, put them together. It was a good job. Very lucrative, you know? Interphones were the main ones in Dublin. They supplied all of Ireland with the switchboards. Him and his brother had that between them. We certainly weren't poor. But some of the others were well off, too.

What kinds of job did your neighbours have?
There was this other family who lived in the lane, I can't remember their name, but her husband was a baker. They were very well off. Geraldine was her daughter. They were really lovely people. They were, shall we say, the 'snobs' of the area! Even though they only had an ordinary house. They were well known to have plenty of money. They were able to afford a very flash car and things like that. He was a master baker. That's a really good job, you know? It means he teaches other people. They were rich but they weren't like that; they didn't look down at the other kids there.

What were the other families like?
The Hattons weren't very well off. TB was ripe then. So many people had it. The Hattons got it. It was like an epidemic then and people was dying from it. Now it's nearly extinct. I mean these other countries are bringing it in again now, but we'd already got rid of it. That's neither here nor there but then, when I was a kid, that was the main thing. That was what was killing people, not the cancer. They get this thing in their lungs and they start coughing up blood. Mr Hatton and Mrs Hatton had about four or five kids. Nice people but one of them got tuberculosis. We called it TB then. A few of them got it because they were living, well, in conditions that weren't very good in their home.

What do you mean?
Well, they didn't have a garden for a start. They had a sort of very small, what shall we say, yard? It wasn't very

33

hygienic. They had problems with the drains and that's all it
takes, something like that, and you can catch it, you see?
Whereas we had a garden.

What was it like?
It was a big garden, a huge big garden that we ran around
in. There was a lying big old tree there and there was an
apple tree. Different altogether than some of them. But I
was one of them, you know?

So, you got on well with the local kids?
Oh, of course, yeah! We sometimes played in the garden
but mainly in the lane. You know, we had lots of fun with
the kids next door down the lane. There was a lane that, you
know, all the kids shared. We'd all do what's there, you
know? And I was doing the singing then, even, and they
loved that. And me and Patricia - that's one in Australia -
no, the one that's in Canada now, she and I played tricks on
all the kids.

What kind of tricks?
Well, I remember we saw this thing in one of the
magazines, the comics, right, about 'Cat Woman'. Well, me
being a bullshitter like I was, I said 'That's nothing, we've
got Cat Woman living here!' They said, 'You haven't!' I
said, 'Yes, we have!' Well they don't believe it anyway. So,
I got her to dress up, my sister Patricia. She dressed up as
Cat Woman. We got these gloves that my mum had, black
gloves up to here on her arm which made her look really
good. And also, things on her head and all. Cat ears.
Anyway, she was up at a window - massive house - and
from the garden you could look up at this window, you see?
We had it all arranged, her and me. I said, 'Watch it, the
window up there, all of you!' There was a big crowd of
them. All kids that had come to see. Only very young kids.
Anyway, 'You watch her, the cat woman here,' I said, and
she came on the window and she lifted her arms and they

all shit themselves. They all bloody took off!

Do you remember any other tricks you played on your friends?
Another time, I told all the kids, right, to come the next morning because I had built a rocket and we were all going to the moon. So, they all went back to their parents and they said, 'We've got to get in bed early tonight,' they said. 'Why is that?', 'It's because Ronnie O'Connor is taking us to the moon tomorrow! He's got a rocket built and we're all going.' 'That's good to know,' they said, 'thanks for telling us.' Well, we didn't go to the moon, did we. I'd built this thing from all bits of wood and stuff, but they all believed it. Whatever I said, they believed. They were all excited. They all tried to get in it but there was not enough room. They were arguing who was going to go up first. They were disappointed it didn't take off, mind!

Did you have friends you were particularly close to?
Well, they were all friends, really, but there was one chap, I remember. Once I looked at him and he looked at me we'd go into fits of laughter! I still remember his name, what's his first name? Jo. Jo Heshan. Now, Jo had this thing about him: his neck was bent to the side. I said to him, "How d'you get like that?' 'I don't know,' he said, 'I woke up one morning, and it was like that.' He said. A whole load of rubbish! But he didn't care about it. Him and I had something between us. We would be in fits all the time. We'd write things down, in school, like 'spiders' ankles', 'frogs' teeth' - all crazy stuff. Things that don't exist. I'd send one off to him and he'd send one back with crazy things on it as well. Of course, when he saw what I'd written then that would be it - fits of laughter! They tried to move us to the other side of the classroom, but it didn't work. As soon as I looked at him and he looked at me that was it. Lovely, lovely lad. I often wonder - is he still around now, what's he doing, you know?

35

What else did you and your friends do?
The kids around there, you know, they were terrific.
Whatever I said, they believed.

So, you were the ringleader?
I was really, I suppose. I mean I was into, very much into
frogs and toads and all like that, you know? I loved those
things. The bullfrog, he was my favourite - he was lovely,
he was. We used to have some races with them. We had
about eight of them around there. It was that sort of area I
suppose. About half a dozen of us and one frog would be
for each of us, and a chalk mark across to see who'd win
and all. There was one chap there: a bad one he was. He
didn't love them at all. He ended up killing one of them. He
stood on it and killed it deliberately. He squashed the poor
thing. He had a nasty streak in him, he had. And after that
I'd never, Frank Hatton he was called, I would never talk to
him again. Never. Because I loved them, you know? Frogs -
they're such lovely creatures. I used to tell them everything.
I loved them so much I sent them to school with me. In my
pocket. Just as you do, you know! And, of course, they go
'rrb rrb' - the noise they make, you know? - 'rrb rrb' they do.
There was one in each pocket in my shorts. Little shorts I
had, so I was really pushing my luck. And I had them in the
desk, you see?

What happened?
Well of course, they started, didn't they? Making this noise.
And the teacher said, 'What's that?' And I said, 'I don't
know, I can't hear anything.' And the other kids were all
laughing their head off. They knew what it was all about, of
course. They knew what I was like, frog mad, you know? I
thought I'd get away with it, but the teacher said,
'O'Connor, come here!' 'What sir?' I said, 'I haven't done
anything!' 'Yes you have - what are you up to?' I took
them home with me, but he said, 'Don't you ever again…

36

grr grr'. I wasn't going to let him have them, don't you worry about that. They were my friends and that was it.

What else did you get up to?
There was a woman we used to call the witch. She wasn't a witch, but we used to call her that. To get to her, you had to go up this wall and along the thing, right? If you didn't do it well, you could fall into her garden. She used to dress all black, so, in our minds, of course, she was a witch. What we were after was these apples. There was a little apple tree. It had these lovely little apples. This was a test if you wanted to show how brave you were. 'Who's going to go next?' 'Err, not me!' 'Shall I go?' 'Alright, go on then, go on then Ronald!' I said, 'Alright, I will.' I was the brave one, so I got up the thing to have a go. You had to climb up quite a bit and then you went along this ledge and at the end of it was the tree, the apple tree, you see? But, of course, she used to come out of her house, didn't she? You can't blame her. 'What are doing brr grrr grr?' 'Quick, run! Cor, you were lucky that time!'

Were you all scared of her?
Oh yeah, as far as we were concerned, she was a witch. Of course, she had this brush, this broom, which completed it as far as we were concerned. Just for doing the garden and that but when we saw it that was it, straight away, oh yeah - a witch! She was probably quite an innocent lady, really, but you know what kids are like, their imagination.

Did you have any toys?
Not really. One or two. I remember my dad actually, on one of those rare occasions, he built me some stilts. So, I thought, great, you know? Anyway, I managed to get on with them very quick: to use them without falling over and all, so I went to the lane to use them. And the Hattons, and the other kids, are all. 'Where did you get those from?' 'Well,' I said, 'my father just made them, actually.' I was

proud of it, I suppose. Happy he'd made the effort, you know? 'We'll have to get some of those, they said!' Next thing, in a few weeks' time, the others started getting them. So, we started to have stilt races. It was always O'Connor, always me that started everything.

Why do you think that was?
Don't ask me why.

I just did!
Well I don't know, do I, but whatever I did, the other kids wanted to do. In't that weird? It's just the way it is. Whether it's the strong personality I've got, or what it is, I don't know what the reason is. I brought fun into their lives, I suppose. And also, the fact of the singing as well. We used to get up to all sorts of things after school, together. It was so fun. That lane was our life. I went back years after and went down the lane and everything had shrunk. Because I'd grown you see? The wall, which I thought was about 20 foot high, was down there. Very good times. If you could bottle it, you know?

Did any girls play with you and the boys?
They sometimes played with us, sometimes. They sort of played with us, I suppose.

I'm intrigued.
Well, this is a naughty bit, I'm afraid. I'm talking about nine or ten years of age. We used to have what they called face sittings.

Sorry, I missed that.
Face. Sittings. Some of the girls, especially the big ones like Noreen Hatton - she had a good big bum in her - they did the face sittings. She was our favourite but some of the others used to do it as well. We'd lie down and they'd sit on our face. And that was fantastic for us! Nothing sexual. A

comfort, shall we say? It went from there, you know. Then we had a thing called touch touch. We'd stand there and the girls would touch us lower and lower: touch, touch, touch. And it was all innocent. There wasn't anything sexual in it if you know what I mean? It was just do or dare. But when I think back on it now, it was the start of things, I think. But we weren't like the kids today. We were quite innocent, really.

What about when you were a bit older?
I guess it was at about twelve, or eleven. Things were starting to happen down you-know-where, right? Now there was this girl, this woman, I think she was a French teacher or something, who came to the school
about once a week.

Why do you remember her?
Well, for some reason, which was great, really, she used to sit on the desk, right in front of us. But she sat with her legs wide apart. And we'd all be, you know - not concentrating on the French shall we say? 'Cos she had all the gear on, the stockings, suspenders, everything. And very, very, very brief white knickers. And, of course, if you were that age, you were starting to get interested in things like that. And things starting to move, you know what I mean? And it was a treat for us, all of us. And she didn't seem to take any notice. She seemed to be oblivious to it all, completely. We were all - phew! To us, that was unbelievable. She only came once a week unfortunately. But there you go.

It's getting dark already, shall we stop for the time being?
Yes. I don't want to make you late.

Well, you've given me plenty to start writing up, I must say!
It's been fun remembering it all. Before you go, I wanted to say I've been getting these mysterious calls on my phone.

Who from?
I don't know because it said, unknown number, right? And it happened quite regular. Who the hell could that be?

It could be marketing.
Oh no, I don't think so. Quite weird in't it? I was at the - don't laugh - I was at the ukulele club on Monday.

The what??
Stop laughing! The ukulele club.

But you don't have a ukulele, do you?
I haven't, no. It was a bit awkward really, what with me strumming there like an idiot, pretending I had one. No, stop it - they borrowed me one, of course!

What's it like?
It's really good, actually. There's a really nice crowd there. My friend, the one that calls me on the phone, she has said about it as a way of getting me out. And they all sing, you see, as well as playing. Of course, when I started singing, they well all surprised. Very surprised I mean. I made quite an impression. 'What a voice!' they said. Anyway, I left my coat in the car and my mobile was in it, so I missed some more calls from the mystery number.

I wouldn't worry about it.
OK.

It's good that you're getting out more.
I know. Did I tell you about Tuesday?

No, what's happening on Tuesday?
I'm going to an actual choir.

What's an 'actual choir'?
It's a choir. A proper choir. I added the actual, just to

confuse you!

Oh, I see!
And I'm doing a gig on Thursday. That's at the old
people's home. And I said to the lady, because it's the first,
I'd do it for nothing. But, she said, if I go down well, I
could get more. This is the lady that organises all the old
people's homes, so she's useful to know. I was going to do
it this Thursday but there was a clash, because of you
coming and you take priority, obviously. I'll do about an
hour for them, that's all, but it cheers them all up, dunnit?
So, I've got a lot on next week.

That's good to hear.
I know! Now, don't forget your shoes. Oh, and how are you
for mushrooms?

Sorry?
I've got some mushrooms and they won't last.

Erm.
They're organic, of course. Tesco finest.

They sound nice…
Good, I'll get some for you. Just a minute. I'll put them in a
bag.

Thanks.
Here you go.

Same time next week?
I'll look forward to it. Mind how you go. Bye now.

Bye.

Chapter 5

Moving to England

Hello Kevin!
Hello young man. Good to see you. Come on in - don't
want you catching a chill.

Been keeping well?
Not bad. My back's been playing up a bit but it's not too
bad at the moment. Cup of tea?

Thanks. One sugar please.
How were the mushrooms?

Mushrooms?
The ones I gave you.

*Oh yes! They were lovely, thank you. I made a pie with
them.*
I'll convert you to organic eventually!

I expect you will. I see they still haven't fixed the fence.
No, not yet. And they wouldn't be doing it at all if I hadn't
got on to my MP about it. They're coming next week,
apparently.

They said that two weeks ago.
I know. Typical, isn't it? But they did send someone round about the back door.

What did they say?
I need a new door, a whole new door, because, he said this one has had it. That reminded me of that song - behind the green door. Do you remember that song?

Yes, I do.
Just what's going on behind the green door. It was a big hit.

I know the Shakin' Stevens version but that's not the original is it?
No - that was later. I don't know who did it, but it was a big hit for somebody. I never found out what was behind the green door, though.

You didn't?
No. I'm very disappointed. They never even told me at the end. I thought after all the hype and all, ha ha! Here's your tea. I can't believe you have such a small cup - more like a thimble! And you leave some.

What can I say? I'm just not as big as you, that's all.
Are you saying I'm fat?

No. I'm saying you're big boned.
Hmmm. I'm not skinny like you, that's for sure!

Skinny? I'm actually a bit overweight.
What does that make me?

Moving on...
Ha ha! The tea won't be a moment, but we can get started if you like?

Ok. I'll just make sure it's recording properly. Yes it is. Good.
Where did we get to last time?

Well, you told me about your sexual awakening.
Awakening?

That's what people say, isn't it?
Not the people I know! But it sounds about right - when it comes to sex, I'm always awake!

Right.
But I was only young when I lived in Dublin.

When did you leave?
Well, I was about thirteen. Norman, the oldest, he left home first. He got in with this girl and they got married behind my dad's back and went to London. After that, Jackie went over to England as well, I think.

What about Marie?
She got in with Patrick Kennedy, who is not with us now, unfortunately. They moved to Cheltenham in a house that, we found out much later - just a few years ago in fact - my father had paid for. We don't know why he paid for the house, but she and my dad were very close, shall we say?

And Patricia?
Patricia moved to Cheltenham too. She got this job, at a place called Jaeger's, as a model - modelling clothes and so on.

So, it was just your mum, dad, you and Phyllis left at home?
That's right. But my mum always wanted to go to England. She always had a thing about England. I don't know the reason, but she always wanted to go there. She kept nagging my dad about it all the time. So, he agreed to sell

the house and move to Cheltenham.

When did you make the move?
We moved in nineteen fifty-six, I think it was. I was
thirteen or fourteen. Phyllis was only eight. My father sold
our house and he made a nice bit of money out of it. It was
a good part of Dublin where we lived - a posh part should
we say? Also, he took his half share out of his business. So,
he had a lot of money. I think it was ten thousand pounds
which was a lot of money then. You could buy a three-
bedroom house for three thousand pounds in the fifties. So,
he came over to Cheltenham ahead of us with the money,
with the intention of buying a house and, obviously, getting
everything ready for us. He came over about a month
before we did. That was a fatal mistake. But in those days,
you did what the man said; you didn't argue. What we
should have done, really, is all come over together. As it
was, the month went by then we arrived at Cheltenham. I
can still see it now. We got off the train and he comes
running up to us, my dad, and he says to my mum, 'I don't
know how to tell you this, but it's all gone.'

The money?
Yup. All of it.

What had he done with it?
What he'd done, we found out later, is he'd bought outright
a house for my sister from hell. The rest of it went down the
pub. 'Drinks all round, everybody!'. The Cat and the Fiddle
it was called. 'Drinks all round boys!'. He became
renowned - the talk of the town. And, not surprising, he
became very popular. When it came to his funeral, of
course, none of them turned up.

So, where did you stay?
It was Patricia. She was already working in Cheltenham as
a model, like I said. Obviously, she found out what had

happened, and she'd thought we were going to be out on the street. So, she managed to talk this chap who owned these flats. Above the shops they were. She talked him around and got us a place above a cafe. A room for us all to share above the café. That's where we had to live because of him blowing all the money. He didn't tell us but at that time he was living in my sister's. My dad was living with Marie in the house they bought.

Did your dad find work?
Eventually, after a while, he managed to get work because he's so clever. He got a job at an aircraft factory in Gloucester. They were doing, what was they called? The Javelin. They'd just come out - the Javelin aeroplane. He did all the interior parts. All the, what shall we say then, all the good stuff? Not the seats and all that business - the controls and that.

Cockpits?
Now, there's no need for that kind of language, young man!

He was an engineer?
Yes, an engineer. And Norman, my oldest brother, has taken after that as well. He stayed in Ireland. They've got a beautiful house over there and the kids. He obviously inherited all that from my dad - the electronics and things. Very clever. He had things after his name, Norman did. Very, very clever he is. He was I mean.

How long did you stay in the room above the cafe?
It wasn't right really - the conditions we were living in. Four of us in one room wasn't right. So, my mum, being like she was - she doesn't sit around - she got on to the council and we got a place in Barbridge Road. The shops were just there - handy. Tailors and a few other shops there. We were there for a while. But it wasn't great.

46

Where did you go next?
There was this couple, called the Kellys. We weren't mad
about where they were so they said, I tell you what we'll do,
we'll move into your house, the Kellys said, in Barbridge
Road and you can move into our house in Shelley Road. S-
H-E-L-L-E-Y like the writer Shelley. A much nicer part of
Cheltenham.

So, you swapped houses?
We did, yes. That was lovely there, it had a lovely big
garden. It was in a better part, shall we say, of Cheltenham.
I mean it wasn't rough where we were before but then,
Cheltenham was not like it is now, you know? Hesters
Way, for example, had only just been not long built, and it
was really good. No drugs, nothing like that. It was very
upmarket, Cheltenham was.

You were still thirteen, so did you go to school in
Cheltenham?
Yes, I did for a while, yeah. St. Gregory's it's called. Not far
from the church - St. Gregory's church. I went there for a
while, but not for long - less than a year.In school they said
I was very good at art, because I did this lovely painting of
Our Lady. They said I was a very talented artist. They
wanted me to go and be a commercial artist, but it meant
staying in school for another year. My mum said, 'I'd love
you to do that, but you can't do that, love, you've got to go
out and work.' That's because my dad had wasted all our
money. And, of course, we were getting into debt, and they
used to have what they call debt collectors. They'd come to
the door and mum would say we're not in or something,
because they'd take so much money every month, you
know? That was because he was still wasting the money on
the booze.

Did you make any friends there?
Not really, not especially. It wasn't that sort of thing there.

47

As far as they were concerned, we were foreigners. When we came over, they used to have, this is really true, the bed and breakfasts there used to say: 'No Irish, No Blacks'. You couldn't get into the bed and breakfasts there if you were black, or if you were Irish. That's the way it was. They termed the Irish as the same as the blacks. But without Irish people they'd have been in a mess 'cos they're the ones that built all the places - all the houses over here. All the roads. Even Richard Harris, the actor, he was on there, on the Facebook a while ago and he was saying how he remembered the same thing when he come over. 'No Irish, No Blacks'. The bloke says that's unbelievable, but Richard Harris said, 'it's not unbelievable, it's true!'

Did you sense this prejudice?
There was some animosity there, definitely. You know: 'Go back where you come from, we don't want paddies here!'

Did you like living in Cheltenham?
It was all right, but it wasn't the same, you know? You hadn't got the same thing as I had in Ireland. I mean you didn't have that same people, the same crowd and things, you know what I mean? It was different altogether, really. I was getting to my teens then and I didn't know anyone.

Was your dad any less violent?
No, not really. I can remember we were at the table, we were having our dinner, nothing unusual, and my sister Phyllis kicked me under the table. So, I kicked her back and she said, 'Oh, Dad, Ronnie's just kicked me!' 'Oh, did he?' Next thing, no warning, bang! A backhander. I went flying back on the chair, on the floor, an ache in me jaw. And then I did something I never done before. I said to him: 'I hate you,' I said, 'I wish you were dead!' I'd had enough by then.

What happened?

He said, 'Did you hear that mum? What he's just said?'
That hurt him, you could tell. I actually got through that
shell there. It hurt him, I think, because his health was
starting to go then. He developed the cancer which is not
surprising. He was starting to cough a lot 'cos of the
smoking of course. Sixty or seventy a day. The one with the
captain on there - the Player's - with the captain on the
front? They were strong. Of course, they didn't know about
passive smoking then. They can't really put the blame on
him for that. But my brother Norman developed a cancer,
behind his nose or behind his eye, I'm not sure which, but
that was probably my dad's smoking.

Did you manage to find a job?
The only work I could find was working on this farm, just
outside Cheltenham. Gilbert's Farm it was called. And that
was a dairy farm. I'd have to be there at half seven, which
had to be on the dot. My mum bought me a second-hand
cycle, a Rudge it was called, not sure whether they still do
them or not. But that was for getting me to work. I'd work
there until around six. It was a long day. Five days or six
days a week. I used to milk the cows. We had these
electronic things, even then, that you'd put on those things.

Udders?
The udders. Not by hand - I'm not that old! Also, I used to
be on the back of what they call the hopper. My friend
John, he'd be on the front with the tractor and I'd be on the
back standing on this thing called the hopper and I had to
distribute all this stuff that they put on the land. I had to
wear gloves because it was dangerous stuff. Some kind of
crystals - I don't know what it was. If you didn't put the
gloves on, it would burn the skin off your hands! I worked
at the farm for two years.

Did you ever have any family holidays?
No. We didn't have enough money for that. But I wanted to

see a bit of the world. People were starting to go abroad more, and I thought, I want to do that. And I managed to save a bit of money from working so I talked about going, with some people I'd met, we got his plan about going to Europe.

Chapter 6

Seeing Europe

What was the plan?
Well, a few friends I got friendly with in Cheltenham, from
school and that, we wanted to see a bit of the world,
without having to pay loads of money. It was exciting
times, you know – early sixties. A lot of free love going
around if you know what I mean? So what we said was,
what we're planning to do - because none of us had been
anywhere - we'll get the ferry over to France, or wherever it
is, and we'd only take ten pound with us, nothing more, and
we've got to see if we can manage on that. That was the
agreement. I can't remember their names. One of the two
brothers - they were a bit, what shall we say? Not a hundred
percent. Up there I mean. They were both a bit thick in fact,
but they were nice lads. Anyway, they said they were very
keen and all, but when it came to the last bit, they all
chickened out. I ended up doing it on me own. They said,
it's a bit of a risk and all. But they missed a lot by not
coming. I saw so much!

Did you still just take ten pounds?
Of course! I wasn't going to chicken out, was I?

How did you manage with just ten pounds?

Well, ten pound was more then but it still wasn't that much.
I did it by hitch-hiking. And working in the different places.

Where did you start?
I went over on the ferry and I started hitch-hiking.

In which country?
It was France first. I think it was, anyway. I had to do hitch-
hiking because, you know, France is quite a big place. This
chap picked me up and he took me to his place.

That was remarkably generous of him.
Well, we got talking and he liked English people and all,
you know?

What about Irish people?
And Irish people - stop being a smart Alec! I happened to
mention to him that I was a chef, which I was. I'd been
working at in The Ellenborough, doing some waiting there
but also doing some cooking as well. The agreement was -
we were talking in his Mercedes or some big expensive car
- he said, 'I'll tell you what, I'll take you to my place,' he
said, 'on one condition. '

Carry on...
I said, 'What's that?' He said, 'You cook me some English
food.'

That was the whole deal?
Yup. Anyway, we drove on and on and we pulled up at this
lovely place he had. Absolutely loaded. This is the funny
thing - just up the road from there Bridget Bardot was
living.

The actress?
She was living up the road from there - that's how
expensive this place is. This is in Beverly Hills - not

Beverly Hills, I beg your pardon, what's it called? It's a very expensive place in America - not America, in France.

Nice? Cannes?
No. I know the name, but I can't think of it at the moment. It's where the millionaires all live.

Saint-Tropez?
Yes, Saint-Tropez, that's it! Anyway, we went in. Beautiful place - you want to see it. The kitchen: about the size of this bungalow. I was there for two days - I stayed overnight and all.

I guessed that.
Stop that! And I cooked him a proper meal in the evening, right? I mean I really went all out because there was everything you wanted there. Beautiful cookers and stuff - it's like what you see in the films, you know? After the two days I said, 'Well, I've got to go now' and he said, 'That's fine,' he said, 'thanks for what you've done.' And he took me out to the border so I could go into the next country then. It saved me having to hitch.

Which country did you go to next?
I'm trying to think. I was in France for a while because it's such a big place.

What else do you remember from France?
Well, this other bloke picked me up, and we were going all along the coast. Cannes and Nice and Monte Carlo, all around there, and the roads are lethal. There's sort of a sheer drop. Treacherous. What he didn't tell me: he'd had a bit too much to drink. So, we're going along, too fast, on these roads and next thing, I realise he's gone to sleep. Just like that.

'Just like that - ha ha'

53

What's that?

I was doing an impression of Tommy Cooper, remember him?
Oh yes! 'Not like that. Like this. Just like that'. Ha! He was a funny man. He always used to wear a hat, a fez.

And do magic.
But not very well! Anyway, this chap who was driving, right, he was doing about eighty mile an hour and there was a lorry coming towards us. I thought, oh my gawd, what am I going to do? And I hadn't had any driving lessons or nothing, so I pushed him out of the way and grabbed the wheel and we just missed this lorry.

Scary.
Very scary. Well he woke up and I said, 'You've gone to sleep, come on, you know?'

Did he carry on driving?
Well he had to - I didn't have a license then. I said, 'You need to revive - better get some coffee or something.' It was a shattering experience because it was a sheer drop, hundreds of feet on one side and a lorry on the other side. But it was an experience, you know? Seeing Monaco, Monte Carlo and all. My friends all missed it, you see?

Where else did you visit?
After that, I went in to one of the other countries and gradually worked my way round and eventually, I ended up in Denmark. After France, I went into Germany next, I think. I went to Munich and got talking to this chap there and he said they were looking for people to work in this hotel. We weren't in the EU then - so that tells you how long ago it was.

We're not in the EU now.

Oh yeah - I forgot! It was about time we got out again. Thank you, Boris!

Let's not go there again.
Fair enough. So, anyway, he said, 'Don't worry about that,' he said, 'I can arrange to give you a part time visa' or something, which they've got to do. He wanted me to help up in the kitchen. It was called Pancho and Pedro.

Are you sure this was in Germany not Spain?
Ha, ha! It was a Mexican restaurant in Munich I'm telling you! High class it was. Not rubbish. I've never tasted food like it. It was all peppers. So, I was chopping up peppers and onions in the kitchen with the others in there - from Turkey, they were. They did the menial tasks, I suppose. You know - picking up things and so on. But I noticed they never washed their hands; they were filthy. And also, they weren't very nice, either. Quite aggressive, shall we say?

What do you mean?
Well, you know, they were very short fuse. You've got to be careful with them, you know? They'd put a knife in your back, you know, as quick as look at you?

That sounds a bit racist to me.
I'm not being racist - I speak as I find, that's all. Anyway, I was there for a while and he, the one that ran Pancho and Pedro...

Pancho or Pedro?
Neither. They were just the name. He was German. He also owned a load of flats. Very wealthy. In Munich, a flat costs you a lot of money 'cos the part I was living in is one of the best parts of Munich. That's where all the rich people live but because he was my boss, and I was in with him, he gave me a flat about a quarter of the normal price rent. 'Cos he wanted me to stay, he didn't want me leaving, you see?

And did you stay?
Yeah, I was there quite a while. I remember I got ill when I was there. When I was going to the loo it was all black. I didn't know it was. I was staying at this youth hostel, but they weren't very helpful. I knew there was something wrong because I could hardly walk, you know? I was gasping because I was losing blood. Lucky for me, I got to know this girl, a German girl, and she was really nice. I managed to get to her, and she said, 'Oh my god, you look terrible,' she said. 'I don't know what's going on, I'm not well,' I said to her. 'Well,' she said, 'I know what I'll do,' she said, and she phoned her doctor. Doctor Frucht, I still remember his name.

Doctor Fruit?
Yeah, I know! But he wasn't a fruit - not as far as I could tell, anyway: he didn't walk funny or nothing. 'Nicht gut,' he said, 'blutungen im Magen!' You're bleeding in your stomach, so you have to go to hospital straight away. I'd picked up a lot of the language by then, you see? So, I went in his Mercedes - he takes me to a hospital called Frankenhaus - which is German for a German hospital. Can you picture a doctor doing that over here?

No, I can't.
Well, when I arrived, they were all in state about something. I thought, o-oh, what's going on here? I think I've had me chips! I must be about to die or something because of all the fuss. But you know what they were in a state about?

The bleeding?
No! The thing they had put me on wasn't long enough - the trolley. It was just a bit too small, that's all. They were getting themselves in a state and I thought 'Oh God!'. Because, that's the Germans. Everything has to be just right.

That's the way they are, they are very precise.

Did they treat you?
Well, we weren't in the EU then, so I'd have to pay, and I said to them, 'How am I going to pay for it?' But they said 'Don't worry. Nein problem, nein problem!' They hooked me up to a thing - to stop the bleeding, I 'spose. And they helped me there for a few weeks, until I got better.

How did you end up in Denmark?

That was the next place I went to. I worked there for a while - clearing tables, just anything I could get, you know? Always in restaurants. You had to get permits for everything. The Danish people are lovely, but their idea of hard work and ours is a bit different.

How many Danes did you meet?
Quite a few. I mean, I'd be doing this cleaning for about half an hour and they'd say, sit down now, take it easy, don't over-do it! That's the way they are but they're lovely, lovely people. That was in Copenhagen. I stayed there a while to get a bit of money together. I got in with quite a lot of the people there and I saw a lot. If only I had had then, a camcorder. Ooof. But I didn't have, they hadn't come out then, I don't think, even. It's a long time ago I'm talking about.

Video eight?
What's that?

In the sixties, they had 'video eight' cameras that used eight-millimetre film. My Dad had one.
I don't know about them. Probably way too expensive - I didn't have that kind of money. We don't all come from families like yours, you know?

Fair enough.
I took a few photos but where they are now is anybody's guess. I remember I saw the lady up on the thing.

Could you be more specific?
You know, the lady. In Copenhagen. I had my photo taken with my arm around her. You had to go over the water bit.

The Little Mermaid!
That's the one. There was something fishy about her!

Really, Kevin?
Anyway, it was such a good experience, in Denmark. Then of course, I went over to Sweden.

Where about?
That was Stockholm. That was a lovely city as well. All again by hitch-hiking. It cost me nothing. I stayed at a youth hostel which was called the af Chapman. It's an actual boat. Not a boat, a ship, that's been converted. They converted it into a luxury place, and I mean luxury. They turned it into a youth hostel, but it was very posh. It's got suites. Each person had their own cabin. The Swedes, they don't like any rough. Everything is just right and perfect.

Sounds like a nice place to stay.
It was, very nice. But I remember hearing some sad news.

What about?
This sea captain came on the radio and said something about Jim Reeves. I said, 'Oh, can you translate that?' He said, 'Oh yeah.' All in Sweden, and same in Denmark, everybody speaks perfect English - as good as you could ever get. It's their second language. He said, 'Jim Reeves has been in a plane crash.' I went, 'Oh no!' I was a big fan of his. I was so upset. It was like losing a friend, you know?

How long did you stay in Stockholm?
I was only allowed to stay for a length of time because,
again, because of the visas. I had to move on.

Where did you go next?

Oh god, I can't remember. I think I went to Spain. The girls
there, this used to make me laugh, the girls there used to
call me Ronaldo, not Ronald. Ronaldo they used to call me.
Oh, they were lovely, these girls, and beautiful girls too.
And I mean, very big… you know?

Uh-huh.
I stayed at this place - really cheap it was, a few pounds for
a night. Like a little, what do they call them? Pensiones. It's
like a cheap hotel. I stayed in one of them for a while and
that was great. It was in Barcelona. I didn't work or nothing
- it was just holiday. I'd made a bit of money from Sweden,
you see? I lazed around, really, took it easy. It's a lovely
place, by the see there and all.

Did you come home after that?
No. I think there was one other place I went after. I've got
to think it. Hang on now, where did I go? That was… I
think it was part of Germany. Yes, I'm sure it was. I was at
this place and they provide the food, meals, for the
Icelandic Shipping Company. You know, the fishermen
coming in?

Coming into Germany?
Yes. I stayed there and helped round in the kitchen as way
of making myself a bit of money. Didn't do the cooking.
Anyway, they brought this, and I mean huge, pot. Two
handles: about this size.

A cauldron?
Well. Think of it as a saucepan but massive. You could sit

in it.

But I'm guessing you couldn't, right?
Ah now. That's enough of that, young man! Anyway, they plonked it on the table, and I said, 'What's that?' 'That's the fishermen's food when they come.' You want to see what they were putting in there. I couldn't believe it. They were putting beautiful steaks, sirloin steaks, the best, into this thing. Smashing them all up. Minced. Like a stew, I 'spose but so good, you know? 'Cor' that's unbelievable,' I said. He said, 'I know,' he said, 'but you watch - when they've had it, they'll leave a load of it.'

Shame.
I know. Well I went, hmmm. A little white light came on in my head. I said, 'I'll tell you what, next time you do it, can I have a go?' 'Why not, he said, what have I got to lose?' he said. They all spoke perfect English. Icelandic fishermen. They all came to this place to have their meals and all. Anyway, the following week came and this time, I made it. And I put in my little extras. Herbs and stuff. 'They'll still leave it all,' he said. But they didn't - they cleared the whole lot. He said, 'You've got a job! Stay here,' he said. So, I came from just a bottle washer to the head chef. Can you believe it?

Did you head home after that?
Yes, I did. I was telling all my mates and they were kicking themselves. They said, 'Oh no, I wished we'd have gone.' 'Well,' I said, 'you did have a chance.' It's an experience, it really was, an experience I'd never forget. And it didn't cost me a penny. I arrived back with more than I started with, so I was quite happy with that, you know?

Chapter 7

Deaths in the family

After you came back from Europe, did you find a job?
Yes, I got a job up in Stafford.

Up North?
Yes. I don't know why I ended up there. Someone must
have told me about the job, and I went to the interview and
got it. Some weekends I'd come back, by train, to
Cheltenham. It was a place for people that have problems,
mental problems, you know. Not a mental home but
something similar. Don't laugh - I wasn't a patient, by the
way! I worked in the storeroom, taking stuff down to the
different rooms and things. I think I had a room in the
hospital itself, to stay in. That saved a bit of money. Five
pound a week I was getting - it sounds crazy dunnit? I'd
give my mum the three pound and the other was insurance,
you know, whatever you call it - the things you've got to
pay - so I was left with a about a pound, I think. But even
then, I managed to save. I was very good about having
money - always. I can always stretch a pound, shall we say?
Even the coins they've got these day!

How ill was your dad at this point?
Not good. The cancer was starting to affect him, you know?

Did you see him a lot?
Oh yeah. I was still living there. In Barbridge Road or
Shelley Road, maybe. I lived there when I came back from
Stafford at the weekends. My dad couldn't do the things he
used to be able to do and I had to help him. I remember we
had this big, huge water tank thing they had then, and he
wanted to put a thing inside to heat the water but because of
his illness, he couldn't do it. I saw him breathing heavy -
gasping and all, so I could tell he wasn't well. But even
then, he still managed to knock me flying, you know? He
was just as bad as before, I'm afraid.

How much longer did he live for?
Not long. He died soon after. 1962 it was. I was about
eighteen, nineteen, I think.

How did you hear about him dying?
I was working up in Stafford and Patrick Kennedy, that's
my sister's husband, he phoned up and they called me into
the office. He said, 'Pat here,' he said, 'I've got bad news.'
I said, 'What's that?' He said, 'Dad's died.' I didn't feel
anything.

Nothing at all?
Nothing. All I thought to myself was he won't hit me again,
that's all. That's the only thought that came into my head. It
didn't affect me at all, apart from him not touching me
again. Apparently, just before he died, he said all he saw
was these giant spiders coming at him. That was the last
thing he saw, before he died. Huge spiders coming towards
him.

What did you mum do?
She thought, oh, I'm free, you know? She went a bit crazy,
really. She tasted freedom and I thought, wonderful, you
know? She started letting her hair down and doing things

she couldn't do when my dad was alive. But the trouble is, she overdid it a bit. She moved out and went to live with Jackie, my brother. Phyllis was with her. Jackie had got a good job in charge of the entertainment in Pontins. In Morecambe. So, she was able to stay there for a while - at reduced rate, I suppose. Of course, mammy had a lovely voice and Jackie managed to get her to get up and sing. In front of all the people staying, the ones on holiday. And now, it might sound crazy but when I hear this in my head, her song, I know she's still with me. 'How can you buy Killarney', it's called. There's a line in it - how can you purchase a fond mother's smile? When I hear that I know that mum's not far away. Sadly, it was the last time I heard her sing.

What happened?
She wasn't all that well when I saw her at Pontins that weekend. She did tell me that she'd had this turn. She felt something running up her back and I thought ah-ow, I don't like the sound of that. It came up her spine and hit her on the back off her head, she said, and she blacked out for a while. And she said it really frightened her. I said, 'You wanna watch it, mum, be careful.' That, I reckon, was, not a stroke but very similar. And, she said, these were her words, she said to me, 'Marie - that girl will be the death of me.' Little did she know! My mum was actually frightened of her. She wouldn't even have her in the house by then. Marie got her in a right state. She was hiding Phyllis, you see, and Mammy got in a right state looking for her.

What do you mean by hiding?
Well, she was just putting her in the house but saying she didn't know where she was and all - to wind my mum up. She was a horrible woman, Marie was, horrible. It was like torture - hiding Phyllis to worry my mum on purpose.

How did your mum die?

She had a haemorrhage - a stroke, I suppose. Bleed on the brain, because she suffered from high blood pressure. She was only forty-eight. Caused by my nasty sister. All because of Marie.

How did you hear about it?
Well, I'd gone back up to Stafford on the Sunday. Next thing, on Monday, I got a call saying that she'd gone. I was devastated. Devastated. About her going. She was such a lovely person - too good for him. Much too good for him. I didn't know what to do. I was lost, completely, you know?

So, you came back to Cheltenham?
I came back, obviously, and I was staying at my sisters, Marie's. I didn't see my mum. I didn't want to. I was in too much of a state. Too upset. I was getting panic attacks, very bad because of it. I thought I was going to die. Jackie, my brother, had come back from Australia. He was there. I got this panic attack and I went running up Hester's Way and I couldn't breathe. It hit me really bad, really badly. My brother Jackie ran after me, 'cos he didn't know what the hell was going on. He said, 'What's wrong?' I said, 'I can't get my breath, I can't breathe Jackie, I think I'm going to die! I didn't know what I was doing, I really don't.' I wanted to die, really. I didn't want to be around without her. Jackie came after me and cuddled me and said, 'I know how you feel' and that was it really. I went to see the psychiatrist afterwards because I was really bad and he said, 'What it is,' he said, 'that's your way of saying that you want to join your mum.' It affected me terrible because I loved her, you know?

So, you missed the funeral?
Yes, I never went to the funeral. I never went to my dad's funeral either, but then I wouldn't have anyway. Marie went, apparently, to my dad's funeral but then she idolised him. There was some problem at the burial. I don't know

64

what it was, between Marie and my mum. Marie tried to jump into the grave or something, all dramatic. She was a fruitcake. You don't want to meet her. I think she's gone now, anyway.

How were your brothers and sisters affected by your mum dying?
Norman was the most affected. I remember we were looking at some of her clothes and he broke down. He said, 'Look at those - the stuff in her wardrobe. All her clothes!' He started crying and all. Yeah. It was horrible. I think she meant a lot to all of us, you know? She was the good one. She was a loving person to us, not our dad. She made it feel safe - the world, I mean.

What happened after your mum died?
Marie, being the 'nice' girl she is, decided to clear the whole place. Mammy was hardly even cold in the grave and what she did was, she locked the house up, in Barbridge Road, no, Shelly Road - we'd moved by then, of course after we did the swap. What Marie did - well, she wouldn't let me in. She wouldn't let me back in to get all my clothes even. I had to pack the job in, up in Stafford, because I couldn't carry on. I wanted to go back to Cheltenham, near my family.

Where did you live?
Phyllis and me moved in with Marie because we had nowhere else to go. I could have stayed in Shelley Road, but Marie locked it up. She cleared all the stuff out and sold it all. My mum had got a lovely home together, after my dad died. She only took a few months to make it lovely, but we couldn't stay there, because of Marie. So, we was with Marie for a little while. She was married then to a bloke called Pat Kennedy. Pat was alright. But he was a bit of a bully, shall we say. He was partly threatening with things. He was such a hard man, he thought, you know? He'd let

you know he was the boss. He always used to think of himself and the man of the house. It's his house after all, you can't blame him. But he didn't know the half of what was going on, of course.

Did you find a job?
Yes, I worked in a factory then. Spirax Sarco. They're still there, I believe. They used to make parts, you know, for the aeroplanes and all. It was very noisy. They didn't, then, know about noise so they didn't give you any ear things for your ears. They weren't aware of the damage side. So, we'd all communicate with each other by mouth. By mouthing. Because you couldn't hear each other, it was so noisy. I was just working on the machines, making the parts. Good job, I suppose. It was all right. Very boring but it was a simple way to make money, you know?

How did you get along with your colleagues?
There were loads of them there I got on great with. Of course, they heard me singing as well, which helped - when we had the break, you know? And there was this chap called, I can see him now, he's probably long dead now, big built chap called Wally. He had that thing with me, you know, like what d'you call him? We'd only have to look at each other and that'd be it: we'd break up. Big, big, fat man he was, and he'd go into a fit of laughter. Lovely, lovely man. He's probably long gone. But we had that thing between us.

How long did you stay with Marie and Patrick?
Not long. Me and Marie didn't get on. After a while, I moved out and lived in a caravan, on the outskirts of Cheltenham, not far from Marie's house. Not a mobile home - just a caravan. I rented it from a man who runs a dairy farm and he was making a bit of extra money with this caravan on the land.

Chapter 8

The Army

What did you do after working in the factory?
I joined the army. I was about twenty, twenty-one - around
that, anyway. My mum had died, and I felt really lost
without her. I was in a right state, obviously, because we
were very close and I thought, what the hell am I gonna do?
Anyway, I thought - I might join the army. To try and
forget. And that's what I did. I joined the Glorious Glosters.
I really enjoyed it and I was good at it, too.

What were you good at?
We did the training which I did really well in. I had one of
the fastest times, one of the best times over the assault
course. And also, I was one of best at the rifle range. I hit
my target ninety-eight out of a hundred. They were going to
enter me for the Bisley thing. All the top marksmen go
there. To be offered that, that's a real honour.

Who did you meet there?
I met some real characters. The one that stands out most is
the one we called 'The Professor'. He wore these glasses
you could hardly see through they were so strong. He was a
walking disaster. Very intelligent, mind. Highly intelligent
but as for doing physical things: no.

When we started, we had months and months of training before you go anywhere. This was in Honiton, in Devon. And, of course, you've got to go on this assault course. You climb up over this thing - it's not that easy - then down the other side and then you've got to swing. You're supposed to go over all the mud, you know? The Professor, as we used to call him, he grabs hold of the rope, as you're supposed to, but then decides to grab on the sergeant, who was standing by there, and take him with him! Frightened, I suppose. So, The Professor grabs him and then tries to get across. But of course, they don't make it, do they? He drags the sergeant into the mud, the yuk stuff and all, which is there deliberately because you're supposed to go over it, not in it!

So, what happened?
The sergeant wasn't very pleased because he had his best outfit on - for going on parade. It was funny though. It was one thing after another with The Professor. He's such a character. There was another time when we were all round the table. We knew there were some VIPs coming because all the best food was brought out - not the normal stuff we had. The sergeant was there, behind us, watching all of us, what we were doing and everything. Anyway, The Professor picks up this bottle of sauce, a huge, massive thing, full of HP sauce. But the chap before him didn't put the top on properly. The Professor decides to give it a good shake, like you do. Of course, it went up and we had a shower, literally a shower of sauce, which went 'splutter, splutter, splutter'. Everywhere it was! Guess where a lot of it went on?

I'm guessing it went on the sergeant.
Yes, he was covered in it. He was about to blow a gasket! The Professor - he was accident prone, that's all. He reminded me of Frank Spencer - off the telly. The one when he wanted to join the RAF. All he had to do to pass the test

- there was a big board with all these shapes - you had to put the things in the right shapes. What's he do? Gets them all wrong and they get jammed in. Eventually he pulls the whole thing down on top of them! The Professor was very clever but not for physical things really. It wasn't his fault. But eventually he had to go.

What else do you remember from your time in the army?
We all lived in what they call a billet. It's a long room with all the beds. Well you get to know people's habits, don't you? There was this one chap and his habit was to come in late, drunk. You could go down the village and there's pubs there. He'd come in and he usually was late, after the rest of us was in bed. What his thing was, he used to hop into bed. A big leap, I mean. So, we thought - just a joke, you know - we know what we'll do. The springs in those beds, they're hooked. They have hooks all around. And a foam mattress on top. A cheap bit of foam: that's the way they were. We cooked up this idea to have a joke with him, right, because we knew his habit. So, we unhooked the springs and just left the foam. Stuck there, it was, but nothing underneath. And we waited, and we waited.

I assume he came back, eventually?
Yes, but it was very late. I mean, really late. By the time he was back, most of us were almost asleep. But then, all of a sudden, he's coming in and wakes us all up with the noise and he jumps into the bed and shhbbbrrr, bang! Of course, the mattress went folding like that in double! Oh dear, we rolled around laughing.

The humour of the trenches, right?
Sort of. But this was the Cold War. We did training a lot but we didn't see any action, unfortunately.

Do you remember any other pranks?
There was another chap, he was, what shall we say, he was

very good at snoring. And we got really fed up with him in the end, so we knew what we were going to do. Once he was in bed, asleep, nothing would wake him up, nothing, virtually. So, one night we decided we'd wait 'til he's asleep, and when he was out cold, snoring us up, all of us got together and we lifted the bed. About ten of us there. Just lifted it quiet. And took it outside.

Did he wake up?
No! He didn't wake up at all. Slept the night all there, outside. Next thing is, about six o'clock in the morning, 'cos you wake up early then, all I heard was the Sergeant, what the bloody hell do you think you're doing? What the hell are you doing here? I don't know Sergeant, I don't know how I got here! Get back in there this second! Things like that stick out in your mind, don't they?

Why do you think you did well in the army?
I was strong and fit. I was only a bag of bones, a walking skeleton, really, I mean you could see my ribs and everything, but I was really strong. I take that after my dad. There was another chap there - he was an ex-boxer. He was about six two. Built like a brick house. All muscles everywhere. We decided one night to see who could push people over, you know - arm wrestling. He had no problem getting his arm over 'cos the others couldn't compete with him. He was a big, hard bloke - quite mean. I was watching them all have a turn and then I said, 'Can I have a go?'' And, of course, they all rolled around laughing, because back then I could count all me ribs. They thought it was a big joke. But it didn't turn out to be a joke because he couldn't get me over. He tried and he swore and everything, but he couldn't do it and he didn't like that! It showed him up, didn't it? Here's me with a matchstick arm and him with his big muscles. In-born strength, init. That's from my dad. Thin, but strong as an ox.

How long were you in the army for?
I was only there for about eighteen months. I was invalided out because of the migraine. We were on manoeuvres at night time, and I was going 'euuurrgh' - throwing up everywhere, because of the migraine. That was because of my dad, thumping me around, I suppose, in the head and all. Unfortunately, it meant I had to leave the army. They said you can't go on like this. So, I was given an honourable discharge, it's called.

I never got to go to Bisley. I was going to go to Cyprus - I had all the outfits, you know, the proper lightweight stuff they give you - but I never got to go. It all stopped. I was very disappointed. I really loved it, I did. Shame, really, but that's how it goes, I 'spose.

Do you think you might have made a career of it?
I think so, I probably would of, yeah. I reckon I'd have done the twenty years and I'd have a nice big pension then, wouldn't I? But it wasn't meant to be.

Chapter 9

Healing Hands

What did you do after you were discharged from the Army?
After that, I was working in a hotel in Cheltenham. A very
posh hotel. It was called the Ellenborough, near Wellington
Street. All the people were resident. They didn't come and
go. All the people in there were loaded. Millionaires, the lot
of them. It's all offices now. I passed there, a few months
ago, and it brings back memories to me, you know? I
thought, they're all gone, those people. Sad, really. The
guests were all lovely. You had the Hugon sisters - they
owned Atora suet. When they died, their grandson got the
lot - millions - because McDougal's took it over and bought
them out. There was Mr. Peak, who was a solicitor and he
represented Charlton Heston, the actor, in England. There
was another man there, he was to do with M&B Export. He
was a director, or something. They were all very well off.
Big money, I mean. They'd go off for two or three months
at a time, on safaris and what not.

Did you get to know any of them?
I was the assistant chef, but I also did some waiting as well,
so I got to know them all. We saw some actor there - you
know, they fire the thing on his head, what's it called?
William Tell! The chap that took that part, something

Phillips his name was - he stayed there for a while and, of course, I got to know him. Lovely man - not full of himself or nothing - really chatty. See you later, Ronald, he used to say, and I'd say, yeah, see you! There were lots of actors staying there. A lot of the actors used to come, and I got to know quite a few of them.

Why so many actors?
They used to come and stay for a few days, you see, if they were appearing in Cheltenham because in Cheltenham you've got the Playhouse, the Everyman I mean - really important place - and actors appearing there would stay at the Ellenborough. All paid for them by the theatre, of course. And they're not snobbish or anything like that but they like to have the best.

What do you mean?
Well, they regularly had caviar there, at the Ellenborough, because the ones staying there expected it, you see? The real, black, Russian caviar - the best. I got quite a taste for it, actually. I used to take big scoops of it because you could have as much you want. And all the food there was out of this world. I was there for quite a while, so I had that under my belt. I liked doing a bit of waiting as well as the cooking because that way I was able to talk to them all, which I love. I loved meeting them all, you know, making them laugh and that.

After the Ellenborough?
After that I got involved with the agency. If their chef was ill, they'd call me out. You get more money from an agency, for the same hotel.

What did you do when you weren't at work?
Well, I started to heal people with my hands. I was a healer.

How did that start?

73

Something happened. I can't remember what it was. I must have somehow helped somebody by accident or something. I don't know. I had meningitis, which is a killer, when I was five, and my mum got me over it I started thinking about it. Maybe, without knowing it, she was a healer, you know? And I think I inherited it from her. I used to advertise in The Echo: 'Healer available. Any ailments.' I didn't charge - just for my bus fare, that's all. I wouldn't accept anything else. This lady got onto me. She had, what's that thing? They can't move their legs and stuff; they lose their legs and their backs.

M.S.?
No, it was sclerosis - multiple sclerosis, that's it. She'd been diagnosed with it and they said it would just get worse, progressively worse, they said. She couldn't get out of the house, so I had to go to her. Anyway, after I'd done a few sessions, she seems to be improving. For the last few sessions, she was able to come to me in the car. She couldn't before because she couldn't feel the pedals. She got on to the doctors and everything and they said, oh, they must have got it wrong - her diagnosis. They didn't like to admit that she was getting better.

What did you do in the sessions?
I'd always pull the curtains across; they'd have to have peace. There can't be music on or anything like that. No distractions - that's essential. I didn't talk to them much because that would be a distraction, even. What I always did was, they'd be in this chair and I was always behind the chair. They'd close their eyes and I'd put my hands on their head for about half an hour, I suppose. I'd always put my hands on their head, no matter what their ailment is. And I would pick up different things, you know? Maybe tingling sensations or my hands would start to burn. They feel something, of course, as well. They either feel a chill and go all cold or they start to sweat. Even now, if I go to the

doctor's, let's say, my hands start to pick it up. It's like a radar.

A radar?
Like I'm sensing people around that need healing - at the doctor's or at hospital.

Did it always work?
Not always, no. Some people I went and did healing with - nothing at all, no reaction, nothing coming through. So, I couldn't help them. But other people just needed to be near me to have the effect. They'd come to me and they used to sit in my chair, right? I'd let them. After about twenty minutes they'd started to go, phew, I'm sweating here! This one woman I'd been healing had to move on. And it was too far away so I thought, what am I going to do? I said, 'I'll tell you what, I've got two scarves.' I know it sounds crazy and mumbo-jumbo but it's true. 'I've got two scarves, right - I will put one on my pillow, for so many times, and I'll send it to you, and you send me the other one.' Back and forward like that. And that worked just the same. It's unbelievable, init?

It really is, yes.
It's not me, it's Jesus that's doing this, of course, through me. I can also see things before they happen because my mum did, and her mum did. I saw the Apollo 13 two days before it happened. Apollo 13 blew up. Or was it the Space Shuttle? Anyway, hey were all killed, the poor devils, the Americans. Two days before that came on, I was having a dream and it said, on this telly, this is terrible what has happened, the Apollo 13 has exploded. This was two days before it actually happened. When it happened I wasn't a bit surprised.

Why would you be?
Exactly! It came through my mum's side of the family, you

see? My mum's mum was offered the chance of a job in America. She was a nurse, by the way. She was offered the chance with these very rich people to be a personal nun, I mean nurse, over in America. A really good job - loads of money, you know? She'd got all her stuff ready and she got to the airport and something said in her head, don't go on that plane. DO NOT GO IN THAT PLANE, it said. She thought, well, somebody's trying to tell me something. Lucky enough she had the sense to listen and she didn't go on the plane. Guess what happened to the plane? It blew up and everyone was killed. If she had of got on, then she wouldn't have had my mum and my mum wouldn't have had me.

Have you had any other premonitions?
I'm going to tell you this now and it's probably a complete and utter load of rubbish, right? I've got a feeling, and I'm hoping I'm wrong, that Harry and Megan are going to get killed. Because I've seen it - that's the trouble.

What did you see?
Well. It wasn't very nice. They were both shot. Don't forget, he was over there, did some service over there.

Over where?
You know, Afghanistan or Iraq - where the terrorists all are. It came on the telly, saying what had happened and all. Assassinated. I also wasn't a bit surprised when Di got murdered.

Princess Diana?
Her dying - that's something I saw before it happened as well. She was murdered. She even said it herself, in her diary, I know I'm going to be murdered. That was all to do with Prince Phillip - he was behind that. The royal family did it. She was deliberately targeted. She was with Dodi and they didn't want Muslims to get into the royal family.

76

Hmmm. That's probably enough for today, I think.
That's fine. It's getting dark already, look.

Next time, can we talk more about your brothers and sisters?
Of course we can, yes. Before you go, I've bought something you can have.

What's that then?
Hang on a sec. It's this.

A fajita kit?
Yes. I bought it from the Co-op.

Don't you want it?
No, not really. I won't get round to getting all the bits you need. You can have it.

I don't want to take your food Kevin. You need to look after your money, you know?
I'm fine. I won't use it anyway.

OK, if you insist.
Here you are.

Thanks.
You're very welcome. You do more than enough for me, I just wish I could pay you back properly. Maybe next time you come round, I can cook you a proper meal?

That would be nice.
I'll do that, then.

Great.
So, I'll see you next week then, will I?

Yes, you will. See you then. OK, Bye Kevin.
OK, bye. Look after yourself, won't you?

I will. Bye Kevin.

Chapter 10

Norman

Hello Kevin!
Hello young man! How have you been?

I've been good.
You've been busy, haven't you?

Much busier, yes.
That's good. That's what you want, isn't it? Very important. I can't believe they let you go after all these years.

That's the way of the world I'm afraid.
Let me take your coat. Pop it on the hook there. That's it. Come on in.

How have you been keeping?
You know, not bad, not bad. Are you sure this thing is warm enough? It's cold out there. I don't want you to catch a chill: you need a proper coat!

I'm fine. I told you - I really don't feel the cold.
Well, you should take one of my jackets when you go back

to be on the safe side. Now give me a hug, I haven't seen you in weeks!

You know I'm not really a huggy person, but if you insist...
That's more like it! Come in, come in. Don't forget to take your shoes off. Now, do you fancy a cup of tea?

Yes please.
I'll go and put the kettle on. Do you take sugar?

You know I do.
Oh yes, just one, right?

Yes, that's right.
I'll just give it a few minutes to brew.

Thanks. Oh yes - here are the copies of your CD you asked for.
That's fantastic. You clever lad! You are good. I want to sell those to make a bit of money for the hospice.

Speaking of CDs, how are getting on with the Paul McKenna CD about anxiety?
I think it helps a bit, but you have to keep going with it, you know? It's meant to help you sleep. I wonder, as a matter of interest, does he do one on depression? He does all sorts, doesn't he?

He might. Do you want me to look on the internet again?
If you wouldn't mind. Not now - next time you come. There's no hurry. If you get one, I'll pay you, obviously. That might be worth doing and then I can get off those tablets, you see? Do you want something to eat later?

A bit later, maybe, yes.
You're more than welcome, if you want. A sandwich maybe?

That would be lovely, thanks.
Turkey? It's organic. We only have the best here! Cup of tea?

Yes please.
Do you take sugar?

Just one.
Oh, yes. I'll just pop the kettle on then we can get going on the book.

Great, thanks.
There we go.

Ready?
Yup.

Last time, we talked a lot about your mum and dad.
Yes, and how my father lost all our money.

Today, could you tell me more about your brothers and sisters?
Of course, yes.

What do you remember about your oldest brother, Norman?
He was a lovely man. But He wasn't as tall as all of us. About five six, he was. But the trouble he hated being that tall.

You mean that small?
You know what I mean! Despite the fact that he was little, he was very, very clever. A bit like you as well, of course. He had things after his name, he was so clever. He's the one that got the brains in the family. First, he was on his own but then he joined my dad's company. But eventually,

he worked for himself. He wasn't very happy about it, but he had to go because the work my dad was getting was starting to dry up for a bit.

So, your dad sacked him?
Yes. Typical of him, you could say.

Did Norman get married?
He met this woman called Marry.

Mary?
No Marry. M-A-R-R-Y. It's an entirely different name. She was a funny woman. They went off to Spain to get married because if they'd got married in Ireland, my dad would have gone there and ruined it all. She'd come from one of the roughest parts of Dublin - Cabra West, it was called - whereas we came from the very posh part. Where we lived is all doctors' now. So, they went off to Spain because my dad wouldn't have allowed it.

Couldn't he have just ignored you dad?
Whatever they said then - your parents - you did. They was no arguing about it, even when you were a grown up. And you don't know my dad - he would have stopped it somehow. That's why they went behind my dad's back. There was nothing he could do then. He wasn't very happy about it, I can tell you. I don't think he came back home at all, Norman didn't, not after that.

Where did Norman and Marry go?
They went to London. They were living in a basement in London. It's now a very posh part, but it wasn't then. They were there for a few years and they had two little ones. I can't remember if it was a boy or a girl or whatever. The basement was horrible because the landlord never gave them any privacy. He'd come in whenever he wants, you know? And they hadn't much facilities either. They hated

the basement. But even then, because it was London, it was expensive. I spent a few nights there to see him and I hated it there too. It was my first time in London. He showed me round some of the places, but I didn't like it. It was very smelly. Not like it is now. You'd get the fogs, you know? The smog. That's made me remember - I got a job in London for a while!

What kind of job?
I was working in the British Museum. It was after I left the army. With the foreign office, actually. I had a good job with them, so I got me own flat. It was with this Italian lady in a rough part of London. She was a bitch, to put it mild. You couldn't be walking on the floor or she'd banging up with a broom or something: my husband's not-a well, you make-a so much noise!

Was that an Italian accent?
It-a was indeed!

You sound like Mario.
Who's Mario?

From Nintendo games. Video games.
An Italian?

Yes. Mario is an Italian plumber.
Never heard of it. I don't think I like the sound of it. Sounds like a waste of time to me. They're so violent, those video games are. Like video nasties. I've read about it in the paper. They make people go out and shoot people.

Not Mario. He just bounces on people's heads.
That's just as bad!

You were saying about your landlord.
The Italian one, yes. Hated any noise at all. You were

supposed to go around on your hands, I suppose. And I got the flu, as you do get it, sometimes, and she'd come in the door saying, why you not work? You earn money for me! Why you not work? I said, 'Well, it doesn't make any difference. I'm not well,' I said, 'I still get paid so what are you worried about?' Eventually, I had enough of her, so I got another place that was different altogether.

Where was that?
It was in Harrow, Middlesex, I think it was. She was a Jewish lady. A lovely lady. She stuck to all the Jewish things, you know? You can't eat meat and certain things. She treated me wonderful - like I was her own son. Her son was an agent of some sort, so she had all these people come to her house. All the top artists - she knew them all. Frankie Vaughan was one. She said he was lovely, he was. All the ones who'd been on at the Palladium and all.

What did your job involve?
I had to photograph these books on thirty-five-millimetre microfilm. The books we're handling, some of them - you have to be careful. You've got to wear gloves and all. I used to photograph them so that if anything should ever happen to those books, if they got lost, you'd have them on record. Some of the books were so valuable - I mean really valuable. Beautiful books. All different sorts of books, with these lovely covers to them, you know, like leather, all leather, of course. Beautifully embossed things and all. Not all religious - some to do with other things as well. Leonardo da Vinci, and things like that.

How did you get the job?
I just applied and went to the interview and they said, 'I'll let you know.' I know it sounds crazy but it's true - after the interview I was followed.

Followed?

84

Yeah. Followed everywhere for over a week. The idea was to see what I was up to I suppose, to check I was OK. The books were so valuable, you know? I had to wait ages, because of me being Irish, before they OKed me to start.

How did you know you were being followed?
Because he wasn't very good at it, that's how! You'd just see him and this car. It became obvious. I just pretended I didn't notice, you know? Obviously necessary, I suppose. Some of the books were secrets. Didn't want them getting into the wrong hands. The Russians or the Cubans, I suppose.

How long did you work there?
About a year, if that. I couldn't stand London. I just didn't like it. Some people love it, I know, but it was too big for me. And I didn't like the pea-soupers.

The pea-soupers?
You know, the pollution, the smog? They had a real battle. They say there's pollution now but there's not. But there was then. It was so bad, when I came back from work, the only way I could find my way along was going by the railings because you couldn't see your hand in front of you. The bus got me a certain way, from Streatham, I think it was, but I had to walk the rest of the way. I remembered where all the things are, and I felt my way back to my digs - the place I was living. Unless I remembered which way it was, by the railings and things, I would never have got back. That's how thick the fog was. It was all pollution. I was healthy but probably someone who had problems - asthma, or something - would find it hard. Everyone had open fires and all, that was the trouble.

Did Norman and Marry stay in London?
No, they moved to Dublin. They couldn't stand it in that basement anymore. He got a good job as well and

eventually got this house, a three-bedroom house, just outside Dublin. Glasnevin was the place. Lovely garden. They had another two children there. I went over there loads of times. I made myself very popular there because I blocked their loo! I put too much paper down. They had to get these plumbers out and everything. It became a standing joke after that. If you're coming again, Ron, you're not going to block the toilet, are you?

Did you and Norman get on well?
Oh yeah. He was a good man. And he had a lovely voice but sad to say, he never used it. He sounded a bit like Matt Monro when he sang but he just wasn't interested. It was a shame really because he had, actually, a better voice than Jackie - the one who did make a thing out of it. Sometimes you'd get him to sing along but he wasn't keen, really. He was quite shy and nervous, I think, that was the trouble.

What was Marry like?
She wasn't so nice. She wasn't very nice to Norman - she was horrible to him in fact. Always winding him up and running him down. He had no confidence in himself, even though he was very clever, and he used to work all hours. She wasn't ever happy with him. He couldn't do anything right. She was always taking the mick out of him because of his height and things like that yet he was a wonderful provider and he'd done everything for her.

How did you get on with Marry?
Well, the trouble was she got on too well with me, if you see what I mean. She was always trying to sit on my lap and all. She'd sit on my lap and you know what would happen then - shwing! Making suggestions and things, because I'm quite well endowed down there and Norman, unfortunately, isn't, and she used to take the mickey out of him about things like that and all. She was a bit crude really but then, where had she come from, the roughest part of

Dublin, so what do you expect? Norman was there but she'd do this in front of him, you know? I felt sorry for him, really.

Did they stay living in Dublin?
Yes, they stayed together until one day, we had this thing saying he'd had this stroke. He got very sick and he went, poor man.

Did you go over to Dublin for the funeral?
No, I didn't want to. I was in England anyway, so it wasn't a matter of getting on a coach. He was over in Ireland, you see? I wanted to remember him as he was, really.

And you don't like funerals.
You're right. I really don't like funerals.

Chapter 11

Jackie

Tell me about your other older brother Jackie.
Jackie was my mum's favourite of the boys. He was
everything to her, she couldn't find any fault with Jackie at
all. He was her blue-eyed boy, should we say? Not Norman
and not me - the one she spoilt was Jackie. He was her idol.
He couldn't do anything wrong. That's the way she
thought.

How did you get on with Jackie?
Jackie and I were quite close. We used to have wrestling
matches, him and me, which was quite funny because he
was much bigger than me, obviously, being that much
older. It was nothing nasty, just joking with each other like
you see lion cubs on the telly. He took up Judo for a while
and he showed me a bit of it, you know, and I loved it.

He could sing as well, couldn't he?
Yes, we could all sing. He entered in these competitions
and things and he ended up, when we moved to England, he
ended up getting a job in Pontins. He worked his way in
and eventually he was the entertainments manager, in
charge over all the acts there.

What did he do after your mum died?
Jackie was as upset as me. At the funeral, he was upset but he didn't show it as much, that's all. He always wanted to go to Australia so after our mum died, he did the ten-pound passage thing.

What was that?
Assisted passage it was called. 'Ten-Pound Poms'. They wanted more people in Australia to make it safer after the war. You paid ten pound and you can go to Australia. They help you re-settle and all. He took advantage of that. And when he got over there he stayed over there. He never came back, really - only for visits.

He made his good name for himself over there on television and the shows. He changed his name to Dee Donovan - a stage name. And he got an award from the television people for something. He was entertainer of the year or something like that.

Did you keep in touch with him?
At Christmas, he'd always phone. Or on my birthday he'd always remember. He was always thoughtful like that. He'd send me a CD of something he'd done. He loved it in Australia. He fitted in very well with the people. They like the Irish anyway, over there. He didn't want to know about coming back, really.

Did you ever see him again after he went to Australia?
Just once. Much later - mid nineties I 'spose. I was married to Kathleen by then and she'd had an accident that damaged her spine. My sister Patricia invited Jackie and me and Kathleen over to her place in Canada.

By then, Kathleen was not at all well. She had back pains – because of her spine – and Jackie knew she did. When we got to the house, Jackie had the double bed and they put us on this blow-up bed. He could have let Kathleen have the proper bed, having had the accident, you know? Being in pain and that.

That does sound thoughtless.
It was. Also, Jackie was well off by then. He was on TV in Australia with his own show – he won awards and everything - but we ended up paying hundreds of pounds there. We bought the turkey from the shop there, but Jackie hardly put his hand in his pocket. We forked out all this money and we weren't that well off and Jackie didn't contribute much at all. I saw a side to him, put it that way, that I didn't know. A bit of a selfish side.

Is Jackie still alive?
No, sadly, he isn't. He died just a few years ago. There was a lady that phoned - the lady that Jackie was living with, his wife - she phoned me, and she said, 'I've got some bad news.' I said. 'What's that?' she said, 'your brother passed away last night.' I said, 'Oh no!' I was really upset. She said he'd had a heart attack. After that, Phyllis phoned me. I said, 'Ahh, Phyllis, terrible isn't it?' She was obviously upset, you know? But she didn't say it was a heart attack. She said, 'He had an aneurism in his stomach that burst. They can't be both right! I don't know which it was.'

Did anyone from your family make it to the funeral?
No. It was too far away. Too expensive to get there. But apparently, some hundreds and hundreds of people were at his funeral. He was very popular. All the show businesspeople and also he was involved in this other lot - they have funny handshakes, what are they called? Not a religion but...

The Masons?
Yes! That's it. He got very much involved in the masons.

They are quite good at show business - they help you get on, get to know the right people, you know? Hundreds of them were there at the funeral. They couldn't even fit them all in the church. That's how popular he was. He's that type of person.

Shall we look him up on the internet?
Will he be there?

He might be. Pass over your tablet and let's have a look.
Ok. Here you go.

What did you say was his stage name?
Dee Donovan.

Where's Google? Here we go. D-E-E D-O-N-O-V-A-N.
Let's see what we get.
I don't think he's any of these.

I'll scroll further down. Hang on what's this.
It says, 'known in the entertainment industry as The Silver Baron because of his silver hair and immaculate appearance'. That must be him!

I'll click on it.
That's him!

Oh my god, he looks just like you - only much more handsome!
That photo was some year ago, mind. What does it say there?

The ultimate variety performer having presented his versatile act in theatres & cabaret venues around the world.
I told you he was famous! And that's a great photo of him.

Shall I print you a copy when I get home?
Could you? That would be fantastic, thanks.

Chapter 12

Marie

You described Marie as 'The Sister from Hell'.
I did because she was.

What was she like?
Not very nice. Not nice at all. She used to make fun of me
all the time. She used to tell me: you're gonna be just like
Norman. I said, 'What d'you mean?' She said, 'Well,
you're gonna be a little short arse, aren't you, like him?'
She used to take the mick all the time. 'You're gonna be
like Norman, even shorter than him,' she said. But Jackie
used to say, 'Don't think she knows that,' he'd say, 'you're
gonna be a six-footer just like me, don't worry!' He was
always good like that. And he was right. When I reached
seventeen - until then I was well under five foot - then, all
of a sudden, I had a spurt. Because I'd had meningitis when
I was young, I reckon that had slowed me down.

What other memories do you have of Marie as a child?
She was quite pretty but not in the same league as Patricia -
so she had reason to be jealous of her. And also, my mum
used to make a big fuss of Patricia because she was
obviously going somewhere - with the modelling and that.

Marie used to bad mouth Patricia at every opportunity because she was so jealous of her.

What was Marie good at?
I do remember the thing she was good at was ballet. Very good at ballet. I remember I used to see the ballet shoes with the blood inside them. You know, when they go right on their tops on their toes? They're up on their toes the whole time. They put cotton wool in there because when you're standing on your toes, your toes bleed. You had to stop them bleeding.

Was she a good dancer?
She went right to the top in it. I don't know why she stopped eventually. She had an accident or something or it fizzled out when she got married and had kids, I suppose. She used to do these shows. Competitions, I suppose, and shows for church and for charities. That's how she met Pat Kennedy. There was a whole family of Kennedys in Dublin. They lived in not such a good part of Dublin but that's neither here nor there. Pat was something to do with the shows, but I'm not sure what he did exactly. He wouldn't do any dancing or nothing, but he was involved in it somehow - putting on the shows and that.

Did you see any of the shows?
No. I was never invited to them. I would have liked to see one. Ballet wasn't for boys. Not then.

When did Marie leave Dublin?
Marie left a little while before we all did. She and Pat Kennedy moved to Cheltenham in the home my dad very kindly bought her in secret. My dad got on with Pat alright, actually. He did something he shouldn't have done, my dad did, so Pat could get a job where my dad worked. He made these things up to say that Pat had passed all these things when he hadn't. On the indentures or whatever you call

them - things you're supposed to have. He said Pat passed so he could get this really top job. That was at the place that made the Javelin aircraft.

Did Marie and Pat have any children?
Yes, they had Karen and Linda. Two girls. When I was living there - I didn't want to go but I had no choice - they were about six or seven, I suppose, if that. I can still see them, they were beautiful looking girls - they had ponytails. They were alright, nice little girls, lovely girls. I remember the room: they were in bunk beds, the two of them, and because there was no room, I was in the bed over by the wall.

You had to share a room with them?
Yes, because it wasn't a big house - there wasn't anywhere else to go.

What was Marie like as a mum?
Well, regularly, they'd come in from school and she'd find something she didn't like. Next thing - I can still see her now - she used to grab hold of the two of them and virtually drag them up the stairs and to their bedroom and she'd get them on the bed and lay into them with her fists. Not slap, punch. She'd punch them everywhere. How many times I had to drag her off! Loads of times, it happened. She'd of killed them otherwise. One day, I remember, Pat came in when this was going on. On a Friday - he'd finished early. I had tried my best to drag her off them. He came in and I said, 'You better go up there,' I said. 'What the hell's going on?' he said. 'You better go up there otherwise you're going to have two dead daughters on your hands if you don't!' That's how bad it was. He went up the stairs and got her to stop.

What happened to the girls?
They grew up, I suppose, and left as soon as they could.

Then, eventually, Karen developed a cancer. She was in her twenties, I suppose, and that was probably from being punched. So they lost her. She used to smoke as well, so that may have been something to do with it. And Pat was a heavy smoker, but we didn't know about passive smoking then, did we? That hadn't come out then. Everybody thought smoking was really cool in the sixties. I'm not sure what happened to Linda. She's still alive, as far as I know.

How did you and Pat get on?
Pat was a bit of a bully, but he wasn't too bad. To give him his due, he was a hard worker, a good provider. He'd come in on Friday and put his package on the table.

He did what?
That was his wage. It was all in these brown envelopes then.

Oh, I see.
Gave it all straight to her. Never kept anything for himself, except his little cigarettes or something. And by Monday or Tuesday she'd be broke again. What she was doing with the money, I don't know. That's why she was cadging off me all the time. I've always been good with handing out the money. Eventually she owed me hundreds of pounds. Then we had a disagreement about something, and she said, 'You can't stay any longer, you've got to go.'

What as the argument about?
I can't remember what it was about. It could have been anything: she was such an argumentative person. Such a temper on her. Anyway, when she said to leave, I said, 'Fine, that's alright, I'm not going to outstay my welcome.' What she didn't think, of course, when she said that, was what was she going to do without the money I'd been giving her?

96

Where did you go?
Well, I looked in The Echo paper and someone had a
caravan for rent, not far from where we were living. So, I
applied for it and got it and paid the first week's money so I
could move in there quick. Marie said, 'Don't rush, you can
take a month,' but I said, 'I'm leaving at the end of the
week' and she said, 'Whaaat? How can you go?' I said,
'Because I found a place.' That surprised her. I hadn't told
her, you see. That's when the penny dropped - no more
cadging from me. The bank was about to go.

Did you get back the money she owed you?
No, I didn't. I told Pat in the end - that she owed me all this
money. I said, 'I hate to worry you, but she owes me
hundreds.' 'You better have a word with her', I said,
'because I'm fed up with it,' I said. He hit the roof! He
knew nothing about it, and he couldn't believe what she'd
been doing. He didn't know she was mucking about with
this bloke behind his back either.

Who was she mucking about with?
She had this bloke in regular when Pat wasn't there. She
was working in this factory. It was a place that made all
these things for children. They were making coats and all
that type of thing. It has some connection with Peacocks
stores. She had this bloke who was the boss of all of them.
Regular, she'd go into the office and he'd come out all hot -
in a right state. They all knew what was going on. It was the
talk of the factory. She was known as the slapper or the
town bike shall we say? And, she even then started bringing
him back when I was there - if I wasn't working or
something. She'd go in their bedroom, hers and Pat's, and
close the door and say, don't you dare come in. Well, I
knew what was going on, I wasn't stupid. They weren't
playing chess, were they?

Backgammon maybe?

No, definitely not backgammon. More like snakes and ladders!

After you moved out, did you keep in touch with Marie?
Not really, no. We didn't see eye to eye, put it that way. I didn't see her for years and years. Eventually, we came back to live in Hester's Way, Kathleen and I did, but we wouldn't have come back if we'd known she was still there. She made a lot of trouble for us. She'd become a nasty piece of work - even worse than before. She started writing these letters to people - do you know your husband's having an affair? Just to stir people up. All lies. Poison pen letters they're called. Eventually they found out she was writing these letters - the neighbours traced her - and they were ready to lynch her. They nearly ended up hanging her because of the trouble she caused. She broke up loads of marriages, spreading all this poison. Eventually, this copper went around to her about some of the things she'd been saying but it was too late by then. And she was in bad way at the time, not well at all. I can't say I feel sorry for her because I don't.

What was wrong with her?
She'd had three strokes and was in a wheelchair because of it. She had the first stroke after she saw Kathleen again after all those years. We hadn't long moved in and we were driving along in the car and, suddenly, she saw us. She went, aaaah! You could see she couldn't believe it. She had a fit, virtually. She knew that Kathleen knew all about her past. About how she was going with that bloke, the one that ran the company she worked for - having it off behind Pat's back. She thought we were going to spread it which we had no intention of doing. And, of course, Pat had gone by then. Apparently, he went into a tree driving or something.

Is she still alive?
I really don't know. She might be but I doubt it, to be

honest.

If she were alive, would you want to see her?
No, I wouldn't. She's already caused enough trouble in my life. She's poison - a nasty piece of work. The world is better off without her, that's what I say.

We've covered a lot this afternoon - shall we call it a day?
Ok, yes.

Ooh, I nearly forgot. Here's the other Paul McKenna CD you asked me to look for.
Thanks for that. I really appreciate what you're doing for me, you know that, don't you?

I know. I hope the CD helps.
I'm sure it will. I'll let you know, alright?

If it doesn't, we can sell it on eBay and try something else.
That would save a bit of money.

But if it works - even better.
Exactly.

OK, I'll be off then.
Now, make sure you look after yourself. I've heard there's a nasty virus going around. It started in China.

Coronavirus?
Yes. Make sure you don't catch it, alright?

I don't think it's that serious. Nobody here has got it.
But you can't be too careful. Especially when you go to London. You promise you'll be careful?

I promise!
OK then. See you next week then. Bye now.

Bye Kevin.

Chapter 13

Patricia

Hi Kevin!
Hi Dan, good to see you. You been keeping well?

Yes, thanks. And yourself?
Oh, you know, not bad, not too bad. Come on in. Cup of tea?

Yes please.
What about this virus then?

It seems to be getting more serious all the time.
I know. Have you seen what they're doing in Italy? It's shut down, virtually.

And there have been one or two cases here, now.
And in Europe. My friend, she's been very silly, I think. She's gone over to Turkey for a week.

Turkey hasn't been affected has it? What's silly about going there?
Put it this way, I'm not being racist or nothing, but Turks are not the cleanest race. I worked with them when I was in Germany, and they don't know what soap is! I said you

must wash your hands, every time, you know? I think I wash my hands about ten times a day, altogether.

Really?
Oh, yeah. These things spread, otherwise. You see people, coming out of the toilet after the you-know-what and they don't bother washing their hands. It's not fair. It's not fair on the other people, is it?

I guess not.
By the way, I've got the diabetes clinic on Friday, that's tomorrow. Mary Berry, she's brought this thing on the internet, right, with a free sample. And it reverses the sugar diabetes.

Mary Berry, from the Great British Bake-off?
Yeah! It does it naturally. And I didn't know this, but Simon Cowell has got sugar diabetes.

Has he?
Yeah, and there was a load of other people on there all backing it up and one of the drug companies said they were going to sue her.

They're going to sue Mary Berry - one of our national treasures?
Yeah - because they're making the money, aren't they? From the drugs. But she said, 'Go ahead, come and sue me,' she said. And then Simon Cowell, and the others, what about them? They can't sue them all! It's only a sample. I'll try it and if it's good, I can buy it.

Is this something you saw in the internet?
Yeah. I mean, she's not going to put her name to something that's not good.

But are you sure it's real, though?

Oh yeah.

You don't think it might be fake?
Definitely not, no.

You've got to be careful of those things, you know?
I know. You do have to be. I gave my address and all that,
but I didn't send any money.

That's good.
Yeah. It's a free sample. But I suppose, when you've had
the sample, when you get the real thing it's a lot bigger, I
suppose.

And they might charge you a lot for it - so be careful.
OK, I will.

*Good. You OK for us to pick up from where we got to last
time?*
Yes, of course.

*You said that you and Patricia were very close. Could you
tell me more about your relationship?*
Well, we always had a real connection, know what I mean?
More than with the others. She looked out for me, you
know? There was one time, I can remember, she saved my
life.

Wow. Really?
Yeah! We went on the hols, on a little day trip, which I
remember well. We were on the way to one of the seaside
places, not far from Dublin. And they had, er, you know
there's a gap between the train and the thing where you get
on? I was only little. I was getting on the train, Patricia was
behind me, right, and all of a sudden, I slipped. I
accidentally fell down there in the gap. And Patricia, she
managed to grab me quick. And she said to the bloke, 'No,

don't start the train!' She grabbed me and that saved me. Otherwise I'd have gone straight down. I was only little and there was a big gap like that. I don't know whether it's like that now but there was then. She just managed to grab me by the hands, and she pulled me up. Whilst she was trying to do that, they would have started the train. She shouted stop! and he realised something was wrong. She gradually pulled me up and out and, of course, I was covered in oil. Completely covered.

But still alive.
Yes, still alive. She saved my life!

What other memories do you have of Patricia from back then?
We had this thing we used to do: a duet we did together. I found the words of it the other day somewhere. We used to sing it together. She sang as well, you see. Obviously, I had a better voice than her, but she still had a go. We used to sing this song whenever there were things going on at our house in Dublin. Birthdays and things like that. It was our 'party piece' that we did. It went down really well, actually. Whenever we had loads of people coming to our house for something or other, we'd do it.

Did you often have people around?
There was always something going on in our house. It was a big house, you know? Friends and neighbours came round for drinks and what have you.

Do you remember how the song goes?
I actually remembered it the other week and I sang it to Patricia down the phone and she said, 'That brings back memories, you know?' And I said, 'Yeah, I know.' I don't know where the song came from. We must have heard it somewhere, I suppose. I'm trying to think now. How does it go? I did the first part and she did the second part. It was a

104

duo. But I can't remember it. Give me a second.

What was it about?
It was just saying that she thinks she's ill, but she's not really - she's just in love. Oh yeah, I know what it was.

[Kevin sings the first part].
And then Patricia would come in:

[Kevin sings the second part].

That went down well, always. It was called 'You're Just in Love' I think. It really takes you back to the house in Dublin - such a long time ago now.

You said that Patricia became a model?
Yes, she did. She had the height and the looks. She's always been a model. She went over to England before us, but not long before. She came over to Cheltenham to work for a shop called Jaeger's on the promenade. A very posh shop, it was. I guess they fitted her up with accommodation. She was beautiful looking when she was younger, absolutely stunning. She's not bad looking now, mind. Marie was jealous of her. Jealous as hell of her! Marie was only as little short arse. She's about five foot, if that, but Patricia - she's five eight, five nine.

How long did she work as a model in Cheltenham?
It was a year or two, I suppose. Then she met this chap. He was from America and they got something going together. Brian, his name was. Eventually, she went over to America with him because he could get her a visa. Everyone wanted to go to America back then. It was a cool place to go - and the money, of course.

Where in America did they go?
They went to where the cars are made over there - all the

cars.

Detroit?
Yes, Detroit. They went to Michigan together. Brian did
something to do with cars - a job in the car industry, which
is big over there. They stayed with his family, but,
unfortunately, there was a lot of tension.

What kind of tension?
Patricia didn't get on with his parents, I'm afraid. His
family were a bit of a funny lot, you see? The trouble was,
Patricia didn't hit it off with his mum. The mum played her
up something rotten. She thought nobody was good enough
for her son, you know? And it caused a lot of friction, I
suppose. And Patricia is not the sort that would just lie
there and take it, I'm afraid. She would retaliate if you got
too funny with her.

Patricia could stand up for herself?
Oh yeah - more than likely, more than half, I should say.
So, eventually they got a place of their own and obviously,
then, it was a bit better. They had a few children, two boys,
but it didn't really work out over there.

Did you meet the boys?
I think they brought the boys over on a holiday with them
or something and I saw them then. There were nice lads,
anyway. Patricia and Brian stayed together for a few years
but eventually they split up. She stayed over there with the
boys until they were older. But one of them had problems,
unfortunately. He committed suicide, poor lad - but that
was later. I think Brian had some problems too - maybe
depression or something, but I don't really know. I
think that might have affected the boys, but I wasn't there,
so I don't know.

Did Patricia re-marry?

No, but she did get in with this other bloke for a while.
Their job was to decorate houses and sell them. Do up the
places and sell them for a profit.

That can be very lucrative.
I know but something went very wrong.

What do you mean?
Well, all of a sudden, Patricia calls and says, I'm going to
come over for a bit and I'm staying with you. She didn't
say why, and it was all very quick. We didn't have any
choice.

Where were you living at the time?
I was with Kathleen, living back in Cheltenham by then -
must have been end of the nineties. Patricia just phoned and
said, 'I'm coming over.' I thought she was only kidding
because we only had a small flat, this was in Cheltenham.
But she wasn't kidding. So, next thing is she arrives at our
place with loads and loads of baggage and cases and all.
She was on her own and I thought, that's odd.

Did you smell a rat?
I smelt something, that's for sure! But there was nothing we
could do. We had to help her. We couldn't see her out on
the street. So then, she had to very reluctantly admit that
she was in trouble. I mean, a lot
of trouble. Big time.

What had happened?
I can't say, I'm afraid. Let's just say she did something she
shouldn't have done really - she left her bloke in America
to take the can. For the thing I can't talk about.

That's not very loyal.
No. And it was very serious at the time. That's all I'm
saying. She stayed with us for about a week in the end, and

then she got some place of her own.

Did she find work?
She started doing interviews rather than the modelling.
How that started is she got involved with this chap who
lived up in Bristol. He was called Robert Smith. He was an
agent. He had something like two thousand actors on his
books, some of them from 'Casualty'.

Impressive.
Yeah - he was doing really well. He had this house which
had three floors. A beautiful house in Clifton - the best part
of Bristol. It's very expensive there. You can't live there
unless you're rich. It's only for the snobs. On each floor
was its own bathroom, kitchen - everything. I several times
went there because she moved in with him.

Tell me more about Patricia's job.
It was in Bristol. She interviewed some of the top people.
She interviewed Richard Harris, the actor. She interviewed
what's his name, Hopkins - Andy Hopkins, Anthony
Hopkins. I remember I was in the kitchen, that's when I
was in the house, and the phone rang and she said, 'Oh, it's
Anthony Hopkins!' And she put the phone to me so I could
hear his welsh accent on the phone there. And he was on
there. 'Can you interview me at such and such a thing?' he
said. Not when he pleased but when she's ready, you
know? And, believe it or not, she interviewed the man
himself, the one who has had all those things with kids and
all.

Bad things?
Yeah.

Jimmy Saville?
Yes. She interviewed him, not knowing what he was like,
of course, it hadn't come out then. Everyone thought he

wonderful, didn't they? I can still see him now, her interviewing him with this big cigar on his mouth, you know? Little did they know then what he would turn out like.

Was she successful?
She was, yes. She interviewed all these people and was well paid for it. She'd make the thing, produce it and that. She'd get all the camera men and all that, and the TV company would buy it off her and then they'd put it on.

Which other famous people did she meet?
Well, she was actually introduced to the Queen Mother, can you believe it? She knew the chap who ran the London Palladium - Parnell, his name was. Patricia, she got chatting with him because she had interviewed him. Anyway, he was impressed by her, he praised her up, and because he liked what she did - she was a beautiful looking lady and also good at her job. I've got a photo of her actually shaking hands her. She was doing really well. She's got a good head on her, always has. Having said that, she did cause problems, unfortunately.

What kind of problems?
There was a partner, to do with the business, called Karen. She was a partner to Robert before Patricia came on the scene. Karen and Robert, they ran the business between them. Karen was a lovely girl, but Patricia upset her. Patricia wanted the thing all her own, the business I mean, and not shared. Eventually Karen had enough and couldn't take it anymore. I can imagine because I know what Patricia's like. She's one of these people - if you don't agree with her, she can turn quite nasty. A hell of a temper when she gets going. So Karen sold her share off and Patricia took over altogether, with Robert.

Did they get married?

Yes, they did, and they were together for twenty years. They had a fantastic wedding in this big castle. A real castle, I mean. There was a long table and all the posh food and everything. It must have cost a fortune. It was mostly their friends - not so much family.

They were still living in Bristol, but Patricia always wanted to go back to Ireland. She thought of Ireland as it was when she was a kid. As if it was still the same but, of course, it's not. So, they went over to Ireland and had some lovely place up there. But Patricia mucked everything up.

What did she do?
Apparently, what I can gather - I've got to be careful what I say here because I don't want to cause problems - they were in this pub and she said something that the locals didn't like.

That doesn't sound too serious…
Ah, but what you don't know is that the locals were from the IRA. They heard what she was saying, and it kicked off. Don't ask me what it was she said - I can't say too much. Something to do with the troubles. Patricia always spoke her mind, but she shouldn't have, not with these people. They got offended by it and they gave her so many days to get out of the country.

They threatened her?
That's how it was. You wouldn't say those things if you know what's good for you. They gave her eight days or something to get out. She should have kept her mouth shhhh, but she was too chopsy, offering her opinions about things. But Robert knew The Dubliners and The Fureys - he knew them all personally - and this was the only reason that stopped them ending up in a ditch.

So, they came back to England?
Well, they had no choice, you know? They moved to the

110

place just the other side of Gloucester.

Close to you.
Yes, I was in Cheltenham. That's when I got to know
Robert well.

What was he like?
Robert was lovely. I got very fond of him. He was helping
me then because I was trying to get into that show,
Stratford's Got Talent. He helped me do some songs for
that. He played me this one song and I had a shiver up my
back when I heard it. I've never had that with a song
before.

Which song was it?
'Who's Gonna Fill Their Shoes' it's called. It was
something about the way it was - a lovely, lovely feeling,
the way it was sung. I thought, I must learn that song - I've
got to have a go at it. So I did it at Stratford's Got Talent,
with all the actions and all. You've got to do the actions.
Robert loved music. He was brilliant on the guitar. He had
all these expensive guitars - a proper collection. He had this
guitar he bought when he was over in America. He'd go to
America every few months. Patricia didn't go with him - it
was better not to. She had her reasons, let's say. But Robert
went there and he saw this guitar in a shop over in America
and it was originally owned by Mary Lou Turner, one of
the country singers. Of course, he snapped it up. It was the
original one that she sang with. He said to me if anything
ever happens to me you can have it. 'How's that?' he said. I
said 'Nah, I couldn't take,' but he said, 'I insist, you're
gonna have it!'

So, did you get the guitar when Robert died?
Unfortunately, I didn't. Patricia wouldn't let me have it.
She sold the lot - the whole collection.

Where did Patricia and Robert live, before Robert died?
After Bristol, they went over to Canada together and they
got a lovely place over there. I visited them there just once.
Never again! We went over to spend Christmas there. No,
not Christmas - what's the other thing that they celebrate,
the Americans?

Thanksgiving?
Yes, thanksgiving, that was it. That time of year means a lot
to Americans, doesn't it? We all came over together, me
and Kathleen and my brother Jackie. I was telling you about
this before.

*Oh yes – when Jackie took the comfortable bed and didn't
pay his share. A typical family holiday!*
That's the one! But its didn't feel like a holiday. It didn't
turn out at all well, I'm afraid.

What went wrong?
We had problems with Patricia on the first day and it only
got worse after that. We found her very hard going. There
was a clash of personalities, shall we say? Her and Kathleen
did not get on well together. When we arrived, Kathleen
was in terrible pain because the Jeep they were using was
very high and she had to try and jump up to get in. They
really should have got a step ladder for her - because she
wasn't very mobile by then. And Patricia moaned because
Kathleen complained but poor Kathleen couldn't help that -
she was in pain! And Kathleen got her this lovely present -
this Russian doll where they all fit inside the other. And
she'd knitted this lovely thing for Patricia because it
coincided with her birthday or something.

You said it got worse?
The day after, we went to see this woman, who was meant
to be a singer. Supposed to be, anyway. She had the loudest
voice I have ever heard in my entire life. Why she used a

mic, I don't know. She was singing all this blues stuff, which I can't stand anyway, and jazz. Because Robert was an agent, we got special tickets which means we didn't need to pay to get in.

A free night out? How nice!
I know but you should have heard her. She was dreadful. It actually hurt your ears, it was so loud. Robert and Patricia loved it but about half-way through it, some of the people had had enough and they walked out. I was nearly going to go as well. Anyway, after the show was over, Patricia said, 'What did you think of her?' and I said, 'Not a lot.' I told he the truth. 'I thought she was terrible,' I said.

Was Patricia offended?
You could say. After that, Patricia went off into a right huff. 'You can't moan,' she said, 'we got you the tickets and all, it didn't cost you anything.' It got a bit nasty. She took us back in the car doing about a hundred and twenty mile an hour because she as in such a temper. I thought she was going to kill us, I really did - it was country lanes all the way. We got back to their house and she dumped us there and she said, 'I'm off,' and she went off with Robert and spent the night somewhere and we were left on our own.

What happened the next day?
She turned up in the morning in a foul mood. I'd have come back home the next day if we could of, but our tickets were a special price which meant you had to wait for the following week. So, we had to put up with her for another seven days.

How did you survive?
Don't ask me how we did it, I don't know. Worst holiday ever. We used to go out all the time. Kathleen got involved with these people that were doing things to do with sewing

and all - making these things and selling them for charity. I said, 'Why don't you have a go - it'll while away the time.' We didn't spend much time in the house.

Does Patricia still live in Canada?
Yes. She was with Robert, over there, until Robert, unfortunately, got ill. They opened him up and said it's cancer. It had spread everywhere, the poor man. It was very sad. He put up with lot, you know? From Patricia. She's not easy going, not an easy person to live with. He was too good for her. I'm not being funny, but he was. That's what I think anyway. She didn't like that she didn't get her own way the whole time. I don't know how Robert put up with her. But he did for twenty years. She used to get quite abusive with him. She'd swear at him and use terrible language. I've no doubt she assaulted him as well, sometimes, but I don't honestly know if she did. He was a big softie, you know? After he died, Patricia was on her own for a while, but she met another man online, Gregg, and they're really happy now. Married and everything. He's either a big softie, like Robert was, or he won't put up with her messing! I keep in touch her, still. We're still close. I phone her up regular, you know, after seven. I've got a deal with BT - free calls after seven, you see?

When did you last speak to her?
It was about two weeks ago. I'm very worried about her at the moment, actually. I've been phoning every day and they've not been answering. And she never said she's going away or nothing. I tried all last week that's gone and all I'm getting is the answering machine. I'm really worried, I really am. I'll phone her again tonight but if I get the answering machine again, I'm going to get seriously worried that something's happened. I hope and pray that she's alright that's all.

I'm sure she's alright. Maybe her phone's not working

properly. Do you want me to help send her an email?
That's a good idea. Yes, if it's not too much trouble. Let's do that later.

Chapter 14

Phyllis

Tell me about your younger sister Phyllis.
We got on fine, you know, but the real relationship was
between Patricia and me. Phyllis was a funny girl, mind.
She used to take my you-know-what out, you know - like a
toy, can you believe it?

Woah. That is odd.
I know! She used to play with it a lot, yeah. That's the way
she was. My mum and dad would be sitting there, and we'd
be on the settee at the back and she'd be taking it out and
playing with it and all. Stop it! I used to say. Funny, so
funny! But then, she got serious, and she wanted me to you-
know-what and I said, 'No way!' 'They wouldn't know,'
she said. 'Well maybe they wouldn't, but I will know,' I
said. Can you imagine if she had a baby with her brother?

Erm. No.
Anyway, that's just the way she was, I 'spose.

What happened to Phyllis after your mum died?
She stayed with Marie at first, but she got pregnant by some
boy or other. I haven't got a clue who he was. All I know is
Marie, being lovely as she is, instead of backing her sister,

she was worried about what the neighbours would think, what the neighbours would say, you know? She was a bit of a hypocrite really. She said, 'You've got to go because I don't want the disgrace.' That's what it was like in those days. So, she dumped her in this mother and baby home, even though it was her own sister. It was Phyllis that introduced me to Jane. In the mother and baby home, and who had just had a baby as well, was my wife-to-be, which was Jane.

What happened to Phyllis after she had the baby?
She got in with this chap, that was nothing to do with the baby - he wasn't involved. He was called Russ and he worked in Mother's Pride bakery. It's not there now but when we were with my sister's, if you looked out the window, right across there it was the bakery. A huge place. You'd see the lorries coming and going all the time. He worked there delivering bread.

Was it a good job?
Oh yes. He should have been grateful for it. But he was greedy, I'm afraid. Eventually, they found out he'd been selling bread to people that was supposed to be thrown, to make a bit of money for himself on the quiet. He got into a lot of trouble over it. It was quite serious - he'd diddled thousands from Mother's Pride. It went up to court and, because he originally came from Jersey, the judge gave him an option - either I put you down now or I want you to go back to Jersey. It was his choice. He went back to Jersey. With Phyllis, of course. And they're still together now, in Jersey.

What did they do in Jersey?
They started running a hotel over there. As far as I've heard, they started again doing things they shouldn't. They started a bit of a fiddle and they got into trouble. I don't know the detail, but I think she was as bad as him: a crook.

The bloke who ran the hotel wasn't very happy. So, eventually, they came back to Cheltenham. They must have sneaked back somehow. I bumped into them once, in Cheltenham and I said, 'Oh, you're back then.' Yeah, we didn't like it over there. Load of rubbish. They didn't like it because they were thrown out, that's what it boils down to! It got too hot from them, I suppose.

Are you still in touch with her?
No. I've not seen her since I bumped into them. I said hello to them and all, but we didn't make any plans. I wasn't mad about Russ anyway. I didn't like him much. He's just a crook, really. But they stayed together so that says something, doesn't it? I heard from her again when Jackie died, not long ago. She phoned me about what happened to Jackie and all that. I got her details. Well, Patricia's got her details. So, if I want to contact her I can. I might. I'll see how I feel, you know?

Chapter 15

Jane and the Children

You said you met Jane in the mother and baby home?
Yes, she was with Phyllis there. She was in care at the time.

What was she like?
Lovely hair, curly hair. About five six, five seven I 'spose.

Good sense of humour, like yourself?
No, not really, no. She was alright.

How would you describe her personality?
She was quite wild, shall we say? Her parents couldn't control her, so they put her into care. And the social services couldn't control her either. They warned me, before I got in with her. They said to me, 'Avoid her, she's trouble.' She was going around, messing with blokes when she was twelve or thirteen - not very good. They'd had enough of her, the pair of them, so they put her into care. That's when I got in with her. I was, at that time, quite lonely. I saw the baby and all, that she'd had. A boy. He was called Dean, I think. What happened to him I don't know. I think somebody adopted him or something. Social services didn't like it at all because I eventually married her.

Where did you get married?
That was up in Scotland. We got there by coach, I think, because we didn't have a car then. We went to the place where - what d'you call it? The place people go if they can't get married normally.

Gretna Green?
That's it, Gretna Green. We had to go there because she was under-age, you see?

How old was she?
She was sixteen.

And how old were you?
I was twenty-four, I think. We got in with some of the people there, who lived there in Scotland, because we had to stay so many days there before we could get married, you know - that's the law. We couldn't get married in England because she was too young and Social Services didn't want us to get married.

But you did it anyway?
I wanted to help her get away from them, you see? But, of course, by marrying her, I broke the care order. This is what they said to me - I'll never forget the social worker - she made sure there was nobody around to hear her and she said, 'You think you're clever what you've done, but,' she said, 'we've got long memories.' They did warn me, and they were right, it was a big mistake. She was bad news, really. Of course, I regret it but there's nothing you can do about it now. If I'd have known it was going to turn out like that… I didn't know at the time, but she was a habitual liar and also very fond of the booze. You couldn't trust her, you know?

Why did you marry her?

Why does anyone do anything? I felt sorry for her, I suppose. I thought she was getting a raw deal, just like my sister. I wanted to save her, I think. A damson in distress, shall we say?

We should probably say damsel, actually!
Oh yeah. Ha, ha! What's a damson in distress?

I don't know, what is a damson in distress?
Jam!

Very good! You were saying you wanted to save Jane...
And I liked her, you know, I liked her a lot. Also, erm... she was also very good in bed. And I mean, very good. She had the experience, didn't she? And me being a randy little bugger like I was, that was a lot to do with it! Nymphomaniac - that's a good word for her, I think. That was perfect for me, of course, because I was highly sexed anyway - always have been, thanks to my father. It's his fault, blame him!

Did she get pregnant quickly, after you got married?
Very soon, yeah. She got pregnant like that, so we ended up with several children. There was Bernadette. And Sean - the next one to Bernadette. Then there was Annette - which is the one that had the harelip, a cleft palate. Then you've got Bridget. I don't know where she lives, I think it's in Cheltenham somewhere. There's one missing isn't there? There was one other, wasn't there? I'm trying to think now - it's gone right out of my head.

It'll come back to you.
Anyway, we had a place in Whaddon Road and then around the corner on Whaddon Avenue. Eventually we got that house in Ambrose Street. We were there quite a while. It was really nice. We had a private garden at the back - somewhere for the kids to play, you know?

Were you close as a family?
The kids were all wanted; they weren't mistakes, if that's
what you mean?

I mean, did you spend a lot of time together?
It was alright when they were babies. Everything was fine
to start with.

How did you celebrate Christmas for example?
We spoilt the kids, that's for sure! We used to go all out,
Jane and I. Bernadette had a doll's house with all miniature
furniture. We went mad really. We spent on them. We got
them little bikes, which they used in the back garden. It was
a proper garden, you know - all cemented but good for
bikes. And they were safe. We didn't spare the expense.
How we managed it, I don't know, but somehow, we did.
They were really spoilt when I think about it. On Christmas
Day there was always plenty of food and we had a big tree
and all the presents. I remember them opening all the
presents, you know? Lovely, it was. A real tree, not plastic,
but after then, you'd have to clean up the mess! The trouble
is, the tellies are different from how they are now. The
tellies had gaps at the back for air and all and believe it or
not, the trees used to get in there - the pine needles and all!
You'd have to take the back off the telly and vacuum it.
Jane and me, we'd decorate the tree and the kids put the
little things on. We'd do all the food, Jane and me. We did
everything together. And at the back of the garden, over the
fence, was some sort of small church and you could hear
them singing - it was lovely.

Did you get to know your neighbours?
Well, on one side, he was the dad of Charlie Watts, from
the Rolling Stones.

No!

122

Oh yeah, really. He's getting on now but he's still alive. He was very chatty, you know, very friendly. A cockney, he was. A spitting image of his son. He was always on about his son - how wonderful his son was. How he was going on tour. Very proud of his son but I thought, if he's so wonderful, with all this money, why are you living there with our neighbour? He was just a lodger with this woman next door to us.

What do you remember about your kids when they were little?
They were all lovely kids. Absolutely beautiful. It's a good line, you know? I always said if I was a bull, I'd be a prize bull, I reckon, because they're all beautiful. I'm not saying because they're mine, but they are. They all had my mother's eyes: massive, big brown eyes and my dad's thick, curly hair.

Where you there at their births?
Oh yeah. I remember Bernadette nearly didn't make it because they found that the cord was around her neck. Lucky the midwife was on the ball and went up there and undid it, you know?

No, but I can imagine.
Ha ha - but best not to, I reckon! When she did come out, she was a little bit blue, but it went. I'll always remember - they say kids, when they're born, they can't see you - she saw me alright! She was looking all round and she was watching me. And she was very big: nearly ten pound. She was a whopper! When we got her home, you couldn't feed her enough. The social worker said, 'Oh, you're giving her too much!' I said, 'No we're not, we're giving her what she wants.' She had a fantastic appetite, you know, and she was a big child, you know? You couldn't see her crying and not give her enough. We used to get all this stuff - sweetener or something - this thing you make up.

123

Sweetener?
You know, the powder you use, for the baby's bottles?

You mean formula?
Yes, formula! And, of course, then, there wasn't any – well, they had disposable nappies, but they were so dear you couldn't afford them, only the rich. So, we used to have terry nappies which you had to wash in the washing machine.

Did you change their nappies?
Oh yes - lots of times, lots of times. Jane wasn't always in the best state to do it, shall we say? Eventually, I managed to get a washing machine and that was one with the thing on the top. And, of course, all of the wash used to tangle something terrible, not the front loaders like they've got now.

Do you remember the name you couldn't remember before?
Yes! It was Kathleen. Not my second wide, obviously, but the same name. She had mental problems. That's the one I couldn't think of. She was beautiful like the rest of them. She seemed fine at the beginning but there was some problem. She was like a manic depressant, I suppose. She'd hit her head off things, in the cot and all. There was something seriously wrong with her. They couldn't do anything, really, with the mental problems. I don't know what happened. It might have come from Jane's family; it didn't come from mine. So, she was put in a home or something. They wouldn't let me see her. They said if I saw her it would make her worse, which is a load of rubbish. I wanted to see her, but they said, 'No, you'll only upset her,' and I said, 'I don't see how I can.' But that's the way they are, you know? I've thought about her often. I'd like to try and see her now if I could.

What was life like, back then?

It was good, really. Jane and I were getting on fine. And we had good times, you know? Taking them to the park, picking them up, things like that. I remember we had some hot summers then. Nineteen seventy-five and seventy-six - the kids were always playing outdoors or in the garden. And, of course, Bernadette and Sean, they were both spoilt. Spoilt rotten, I mean.

In what way?

Well, they were going to St. Gregory's School, right, and a lot of the people that went there are loaded. They're builders - got pots of money. Bernadette and Sean, they were dressed better than some of those kids. They both dressed like Lord and Lady Muck, the two of them! It was because they were the first two - they had absolutely everything they wanted. Sean had a special coat, done with a velvet collar, and he had a deer-stalker hat, like Sherlock Holmes. And leather boots. All the best of everything. And Bernadette was the same. Sean had all these lovely sweaters, which he decided to give to some friends of his. Some of the sweaters ended up on the top of the school. Money was no object with him. Some of the kids in school who weren't very well off, they would give him their sweater and they'd have Sean's. He'd come back with an old sweater with holes! How many sweaters he lost I cannot remember but it cost a lot of money. Bernadette was different altogether: she looked after her stuff. She could look after herself too!

What do you mean?

Physically, she was way ahead. A very big child, she was. She had a fantastic appetite and she showed it, you know what I mean? She showed what she ate, put it that way.

You mean she was fat?

How dare you say that about my child, ha! Let's just say

she had a solid build. But the trouble is, when the other kids came along, she started becoming a bit of a bully because of her size and all. And she used to bully Shaun a bit. The others were a lot younger than her and she didn't like them getting all the attention, I suppose. And at school she was hard, as they call it. She knew how to look after herself. If some girl upset her, she used to lay them out. Girls maybe two classes above her - it didn't make any difference to her. She was built like a tank and strong with it.

Did you ever sing to the kids?
Sometimes, yeah, yeah. I sang that one, 'I'm Nobody's Child'. They used to love that one. It's about a poor orphan boy – no mummy's kisses, no daddy's smile. 'Oh, that poor boy!' they used to say. It had them in tears, you know? That was their favourite, that one. They liked to hear me singing. There was some good times, then. But, of course, they were still very little when they were taken away, all four of them.

What was the reason?
I think it all started with Annette. Things started to change when we had Annette because, bless her old soul, it's not her fault, she was born with a harelip and cleft palate - but really bad. But otherwise she was a beautiful looking child. It's like this: no roof to the mouth. And, of course, we had a problem feeding her with the bottle because, obviously, you had to be careful she didn't choke. The milk would all go up and come through the nose there, you know? Social services tried to make problems with that, saying it was our fault, but the doctor told them to go and piss off because that's a load or rubbish, he said.

Why did they try to make trouble?
Well, they tried to make out we'd caused it, which is a load of nonsense. But the doctor said, 'That's caused in the womb, you know?'

But why did they think you might have caused it?
Because that's the way they were. They tried anything, you know? It's because she'd made this statement; they used any excuse to take the kids away.

What statement?
Jane had made this statement to Social Services, that's the trouble. That's how it started. She retracted it but the damage was done.

What did she say in the statement?
It was all a pack of lies. She said I was killing the kids, more or less, which I wasn't. Crazy.

Did she mean hitting them?
Well, something like that. I have no idea why she said it. She said I was killing the kids, which obviously I wasn't. They expected to find bodies everywhere, I suppose.

You really have no idea why she said it?
I think she'd had enough of looking after the kids and Annette was the last straw. I don't think she could cope with Annette. It was too much for her. Until then, we were fine. Basically, we just had too many children really, I think, as well. She was so fertile, and I was too, you know? She used to say to me after we had sex, she used to actually say to me, I know I'm pregnant. I said, 'You can't know that.' She said, 'I'm telling you, I'm pregnant.' And she was always right.

She knew?
She knew, yeah. I wanted children anyway - they weren't accidents. I wanted lots of kids, you know, but I wanted to be able to bring them up and not have them all taken off me.

So, what led to Social Services finally taking the kids?

There was an accident, a pure accident, that's all it was, with Bernadette. We were living in Ambrose Street and back then, I suffered from terrible migraines. I mean, really bad - three days out of action with them. Getting sick and everything. Horrible. And I had a really bad migraine this day. Bernadette was eight then. Anyway, she was playing Jane up so Jane called me down to sort it out. And she was being bullied, Bernadette, by the other kids and she got fed up and she shouted up to me to do something and I said 'Arrgh'. It was a sunny day and, of course, your eyes are affected with the migraine. Anyway, I came down, reluctantly - I didn't really want to - and I said, 'Bernadette, come on in!' And she started using bad language, which I wasn't having so I dragged her in, went to give her a smack on the bum, which doesn't do them any harm anyway. And she's built like a fortress. What she did was - she was pulling away from me and next thing is she kicked me in the shin, and of course I let her go and she went straight over and hit her nose on the chair. Wooden chair, hard. And it started bleeding, of course, not surprising. Anyway, Jane saw this and went ballistic.

What did she do?
She panicked, you see? Then, she disappeared, Jane did. I didn't know where the hell she'd gone. Anyway, I got some ice, stopped the bleeding. Within half an hour, Bernadette was outside, playing with the others - all her brothers and sisters. Next thing is, a knock comes to the door, I open the door and it's a social worker and the police outside. What's this I hear about what you've done Mr O'Connor? I said, 'That's a load of rubbish, I've done nothing.' She didn't give me a chance to speak, the social worker. So, she came in and took the kids. All of them. Then went out and that was it.

Just like that?
Yup. Just like that. They said they had long memories and

128

they were right. The girl that took them: she was only about sixteen, seventeen. What does she know about kids? I can still remember her name: Lloyd. Susan Lloyd. This was her first case. Only young but she still had the power to take the kids. Didn't want to hear what I had to say at all. Wasn't interested.

Did they suspect you of hurting the kids?
Yes, they did. She insisted the doctor examine them. They didn't find anything because there was nothing to find. She said, 'Just because you can't find anything, what about bone bruising?' She wanted him to X-ray them, but he wouldn't do it because they were only little. He said, the doctor said, 'If you think I'm gonna X-ray a little child you've got another thing coming because I'm not. There's nothing wrong with these children!'

He said about Bernadette, 'The only trouble with her is,' he said, 'she's over-fed and a spoilt brat!' 'Cos she liked her grub. That's what the doctor said. So, there was no evidence. What it boiled down to, really, the real reason behind this, was Jane couldn't cope with Annette, with the hair lip. That was just an excuse, when she saw Bernadette and the blood. It was entirely Bernadette's own fault because she shouldn't have kicked me, you know?

So, you think Jane wanted them to be taken into care?
I think so, yeah. I think she wanted them, she wanted the kids, she wanted to carry them, but she didn't want to look after them afterwards. She'd got problems and she couldn't cope. I should have seen it. I didn't. It's easy looking back now. The way she was going off, for example. She used to just go off for days, weeks.

Without any warning?
She just disappeared without telling me. One time, she left Bernadette, she was only a baby, she left her on this pot, in

129

front of the cooker. The cooker was on. I'd locked the door
so she couldn't get out and she went out through one of the
windows!

You'd locked her in?
I didn't want her leaving, you see? Well, anyway, she went
off with one of these dosser blokes she liked. 'Cos
obviously, they buy her the drinks. I don't drink so I wasn't
any good that way, if you see what I mean? I wasn't into
booze, even then. I'd seen my dad, the way he was - it
probably turned me off. When she went off, she'd be gone
for two, three weeks at a time. I don't know where she
went. She'd call me from different places. Hull one of the
times, something Island - all these different places she'd
been with these dossers and all. Drunks and all, she'd go
with.

How did she meet them?
Unfortunately, next door to us, in Ambrose Street, was a
doss house. Nothing to do with us - it was just a place for
drunks and down-and-outs and all. She got involved with
this bloke called Walsh. I didn't know this. I didn't meet
him at all. I only found out later.

But she'd always come back?
Every time. Probably when she'd ran out of money. And I
used to have her back, each time, as if nothing had
happened and that would be it for a while.

When did you eventually split up?
Eventually, after the kids were taken, she moved in with
him. Walsh. I wanted to see him, but he wouldn't come and
see me. I gave a message to one of his kids that I wanted to
meet him, but he wouldn't, of course. He knew what I'd do
if he did, that's why. I was very into martial arts by then. In
a way, I regret getting in with Jane because she was trouble,
really was, and I lost the children because of her. If I'd have

been with another woman, none of them would have gone into care. Jane ruined their life, and mine, that's what it basically boils down to.

Did you get to see the children when they were in care?
No, no. Not really. They say they're going to do this and that but it's all a load of rubbish. You get letters but not much else. I saw them occasionally but that was it. And it affected them all. They don't always do it for the right reason, fostering, if you know what I mean. It's big money, fostering. A hundred pounds for each of the children they got. And they were getting their car paid for, their mortgage paid for, everything! They knew what they were doing, alright. They didn't care about the kids.

Did you try to get them back?
I did everything. But back then, they could take your kids and that was that. There was no right of appeal. I wanted to change all that and get them back.

But that, as they say, is another story.
I'm very proud of what I achieved in Strasbourg.

I know you are. It's one of the reasons we're writing this book.
It is.

I think I should be heading off now.
OK, fair enough. Now, I'm wondering if you could do me favour?

What's that?
Well, could you pick me up a chicken? I always like to have a chicken and the mince is so I can make a Bolognese. Oh, and some eggs.

Sure, I can do that.

It's because of the news. They're saying if you're over seventy, you should be careful, because of Coronavirus.

I heard that too.
And some of the shops are running low on a few things.

Well, I'll see what I can do.
Thanks. See you soon. Be careful out there, alright?

I will.
And no more trips to London, you promise? It's not safe. Too many people with the virus down there. I worry about you.

OK, Kevin, I promise.
Good. See you then, bye.

See you Kevin.

Chapter 16

Trouble with the Neighbours

Hi Kevin.
I thought it was you. Exactly on time, as usual!

It's an easy journey.
But it's a shame you have to drive so far, now. Anyway,
come in, come in before the cold gets in. Let me take your
coat. That's a much better coat. Not like the flimsy thing
you had on last time! I don't want you catching a chill what
with these winds and everything.

I'll be fine, don't you worry.
I do worry.

Yes, I know you do but you don't need to.
Cup of tea? One sugar, right?

That's right.
I'll just be a minute.

Here's shopping you asked for.
Thanks.

There's been a bit of panic buying, I think.

Because of this virus?

Yes. You were lucky, this was the last chicken in the shop.
I can see why!

*Yeah, it looks odd, doesn't it? But it's just been packed
upside down. That must have put people off buying it.*
It hasn't been packed wrong.

Yes, it has - look?
No. That's because it's an Australian chicken.

Er? Ah, yes, I see. That must be it, of course!
You should of thought of that, shouldn't you?

Well, yes, but it's obvious now you say it.
I like a bit of Australian chicken, thank you. I have it with
some apple turn-over!

Ha! A traditional Australian meal, lovely!
Here's your tea.

Thanks. Good to go?
Yes.

*OK, let's see where we got to. Ah yes. You mentioned that
you learned martial arts when you were with Jane. What
got you started?*
I wanted to make sure I could look after myself, really, and
the kids. I remember one time signing on in the labour
exchange in St. Paul's Street, and there was this gypsy in
the queue. I was in front and he said to me, 'Do you mind
moving?' And I said, 'No, I'm in the queue, you've got to
wait your turn.' But he didn't like it - being told. I didn't
think any more of it. Anyway, he disappeared but I had to
take ages filling in these papers and all sorts of thing, you
know, to get work. Then after, when I come out, this van

opened, and about six of them, out and out gypsies they were, came out of the van. He'd got on to them and said I'd called him a dirty gypo - which I hadn't, by the way. He'd convinced them as a way of getting his own back. He'd riled them up, telling them a pack of lies. So, they came out of the van and they had chains, bicycle chains, which was a very popular weapon then. They were going to beat the shit out of me. They meant business. And none of the people around were prepared to interfere or to help - they'd only get involved, right?

What did you do?
I legged it! I thought better than getting my head kicked in. After that, I thought to myself, I don't want to get in that situation again if I can avoid it. I realised if you can't look after yourself, nobody else is going to help you. And as things would happen, a few days later, in The Echo I saw this club in Whaddon Road: The Whaddon Boys ClubThey were opening a thing for beginners for Karate. I thought, I'll go and have a go. So, I went along and got a few bruises here and there.

Sounds painful.
It was. There was big chap, higher up than me, an ex-copper or something, built like a fridge and he did the damage. He was coming up with these full kicks all the time, which he shouldn't have, really. You're supposed to stop them, the kicks, before they hit hard, you know what I mean? I had to keep blocking. Block, block, block all the time so I got bruised and all, but I thought it was better than having my ribs kicked in. He was a bully, really. It wasn't a namby-pamby place, shall we say? Jane said, 'You're not going back; you can't go back - look at the bruises you've got!' But I said, 'Oh yes I am.' I remembered the gypsies attacking me and I kept that in my mind.

You were clearly determined to toughen up.

I wanted to make sure I could defend myself, that's all. It was a hard way of learning, but it teaches you how to block properly. Anyway, gradually I got a bit better at it. A few months went by and I was getting quite good then and guess who I saw again? The same bloke and two or three of them outside the labour exchange. But this time they said, 'Oh hi, how are you? You alright?' They were all over me; no bother at all. It just shows you the difference if you give off something.

Like a skunk?
No! I mean if you come across all confident. And also, it's the eyes. It shows in the eyes that you're not to be messed with. I never had trouble there, after that.

Have you ever had to use your karate skills in real life?
Yes, yes, I have, once or twice. I remember I had to defend myself when we were in our little house in Whaddon Avenue. We had this neighbour - he was a funny man. An arrogant little shit - excuse my language. What he kept doing was, because the way the doors were put on - the hinges were on the wrong side - when his door slammed, you really heard it. And the kids were only little; one was only a baby, trying to sleep and all. Anyway, he was doing something to do with his car, and he was in and out, in and out and I got fed up with it. This was on a Sunday as well. Eventually, I'd had enough so I said, 'Brian, would you mind not slamming that door all the time?' I said, 'I've got little ones here and they're trying to get to sleep.' Anyway, he didn't take it nice. He had this spanner, a big bloody thing for the car, and he got quite nasty with me. He decided to try and rearrange my head with it. But I'd learnt how to block, so I blocked it a few times on my arm rather than on my head and then I retaliated.

What did you do?
I gave him a right beating. I broke his nose with a few

136

punches, blacked both his eyes, knocked a few of his teeth out etc. etc. I was only defending myself. His grandmother said, 'I'm gonna call the police, look what you've done to my grandson!' 'I'm not interested,' I said, 'he deserved what he got.' She couldn't go to the police because he attacked me, you know, and I had the bruises to prove it.

Was he OK?
Well, he had a sore head for a while, to say the least, but he recovered eventually.

What about you?
Well, I went to the hospital but only 'cos Jane said go to the hospital. I didn't want to bother. And there was this black guy, a lovely Jamaican, and I told him what happened, and he said, 'Whaaat? You mean you blocked it with your arm?' I said, 'Yeah, I did.' And he said, 'You must be made of steel!' I still remember him saying that. He checked me and there was no damage.

You were lucky.
Not really. I knew what I was doing, you see, thanks to the martial arts. And a similar thing happened with this other chap at our next place because I wouldn't put up with his messing. He tried to attack me with this thing, I forget what it was now - something nasty, a machete I think it was. If it wasn't for the karate, I wouldn't be around now.

If my dad had lived a bit longer, I would have eventually... well, we would have had a hell of a fight. After I'd learnt martial I arts I didn't put up with anyone's messing. If someone messed with me - big mistake.

Do you think learning martial arts changed you?
It made me more confident, I think. It meant I was in control. I wasn't going to pushed around by anyone. But my sister Marie didn't like it. She wrote to Jackie, my

137

brother, saying she didn't like the way I'd changed, because I was looking after myself and I stood up to her husband, Patrick. When I lived with them, he was terrible, you know, always picking on me all the time, threatening me and everything. He thought martial arts was a load of rubbish, but it wasn't a load of rubbish - it saved my life a few times. I remember, we were in one of the supermarkets and he said something to me, and I said, 'If you say anything like that again you'll end up in that freezer.' I was angry with him for making fun of me, but he never retaliated because, well, he knew, didn't he, what I was capable of?

Which martial arts did you learn?
Karate, of course. I also learnt a bit of Judo from Jackie, my brother. And I learnt Taekwondo, but I wasn't very impressed with that. I didn't like it - it was too slow. They'd use such a long warm up. You're wasting time, I thought, when you could be practising and blocking. It was only my opinion, but that's why I didn't take to it. Then I did Kung Fu. I got into that because Sean, my son, was into that. I did that for a while and that was good.

What does Kung Fu involve?
It's not so aggressive as karate, it's more subtle. The last one I did, which I'm thinking of doing again, is Wing Chun. I like it very much and there's a good club in Stratford. But not now. When things are more settled shall we say. Maybe if Kathleen and I talk, you know, and I feel better about myself, then I'll do it.

What's special about Wing Chun?
It's amazing. It's all about the hands and moving your body. Just your hands, no kicking or nothing. You're moving and your body's swaying out of the way and you're using your arms and blocking. It's very good against weapons. It was invented by a nun. She invented it because of the long skirts they wear - skirts right down to their feet. She couldn't do

138

the kicks, you see?

That does make sense!
This is what they say - I don't know whether it's true or not.
It happened hundreds of years ago or thousands of years
ago, apparently. She went up a mountain, as they do, and
started thinking about what to do and then she came down
from the mountain and she had this new form of martial
arts. It's the one Bruce Lee became popular with. You don't
have to wear outfits; you can just put an old t-shirt on
whereas the Karate is expensive. You have to buy two or
three outfits and they cost you a lot of money.

Have you ever regretted using your martial arts abilities?
I don't think so, no. I never hit anybody who didn't have it
coming to them. Some people need to be taught a lesson,
you know?

Maybe.

Chapter 17

Bernadette

Did your children all get taken to the same foster home?
They should have been, but they weren't. Bernadette and
Sean, they were in the same place, but others were in
different foster homes - they split them all up, which they
shouldn't have done, really. That hit them hard, I think.

Were they well looked after?
I'm afraid not, no, they weren't. Bernadette and Sean went
in with Mr. and Mrs. Creswell. That was Swindon village,
which is the outskirts of Cheltenham. They fostered a load
of other children there as well, but they were in it for the
money. And apparently, he'd go around, Chris Creswell he
was called, he'd be paying the girls to keep quiet.

Keep quiet about what?
He was messing about with them, interfering with all the
girls, including Bernadette. I didn't know anything about it
until it all came out. He paid them so much just to keep
quiet. Eventually, one of the girls accidentally let it slip and
said something and then they took him, and it all got out.
He'd been doing this for years, apparently. Eventually, it
came to light and he went to court and, believe it or not, the
social services spoke up for him and praised him up. They

gave him a glowing reference, saying what a wonderful man he was, how he'd fostered for all these years. Nothing about the damage he'd done. That's what they're like - they've got double standards. They put him down, but only a few months. But there you are. Of course, that didn't do Bernadette any good. I've told her to take Mrs Creswell, the husband's dead now, to court, for damages and all. It doesn't matter how long ago it was. Take her for the money she's got, and she's got lots - three houses all bought with miserable money. But she won't. It's silly, but she won't.

So, they must have found Bernadette and Sean a new foster home?
No, they went back to the same place, would you believe it?

That's awful.
So, Bernadette had to go back to where it all happened. Mrs. Creswell took over the place and kept all the kids. She reckoned she knew nothing about it, which I don't believe - a complete pack of lies.

How was Bernadette affected?
I don't know if it was the foster home or because of the bloods from my dad, through me, that Bernadette was so vindictive. So angry all the time. She holds grudges. Bernadette was laying kids out, if they got funny with her. Bernadette, I'm afraid she has a very, very nasty temper when she gets going.

What did she do when she left the foster home?
They must have found her a flat or something - I don't know what it was: they wouldn't tell me anything. Once they're into care, that's the way it is.

When did you see her next?
I found out she was living in this place in Cheltenham - a little house. She must of wrote me a letter or something

because I didn't know where she was. But she didn't like it there because around that area there was a lot of trouble with the blacks. There was riots and all. A hell of a lot of trouble with the blacks and it was getting quite vicious. She said, 'I'm not going to stay here,' she said, 'I can't stand this much longer, dad, I've got to get out of this environment.' 'I don't blame you,' I said, 'we'll look out for a place.' And eventually, she managed to get another place because she got in with this chap. She was very lucky really because this bloke that she got in with, Martin his name was, he changed her life. He was loaded and I mean loaded. And he managed to get her this little house that she stayed in for several years. She got pregnant off him - Emily, that's his daughter. Eventually her and Martin split up. I've only heard her side; I'd like to hear his side as well. Then she lost the house. I think what happened is she had too many things on the mortgage, including her car, and couldn't keep up the payments.

What did she do?
After that, she met Andy. He works at the Gloucester hospital, helping people round in the wheelchair sort of things - so they can get to operations and that. What do you call a person like that? Orderly or something, I 'spose it is. He doesn't do any nursing, anyway. She had a little boy, Morgan, off Andy. And eventually, after she got divorced, Bernie got married to Andy.

Did having children calm her down?
Oh no. She didn't change at all. One day I found a scratch on her car. Somebody maybe done it when it was parked at the shops? Anyhow, I pointed it out to her, next thing is she went ballistic, virtually. She went in and started onto Andy. It was nothing to do with him! The temper - wow! I know where it comes from. It comes from my dad. As she's getting older, she's getting more and more like him and my sister Marie. I'm afraid that's come into her. These things

142

do, don't they? I'm the first to admit, I've got a hell of a temper, when I get going, as well. But I've managed to control it because I knew what my father was like. You've got to allow for the fact that Bernadette, she was in that foster home. That didn't help. With that foster father, you know - what he was doing and all.

How did you get along with Bernadette?
Fine to start with, but then I didn't hear from her for ages after I got in with Kathleen. Bernadette went off as soon as Kathleen came onto the picture. She wrote a letter to me and she said, 'Don't come to my wedding or I'll cancel it. You and Kathleen are very boring.' Or something like that. She didn't want to know about us, she said, and I never heard any more of her for twelve years.

Twelve years?
Didn't see her, didn't hear from her all that time.

Why was she so angry with you?
She's got problems, unfortunately, you know? I don't know what makes her think. I don't know what the reason was, I'll never find out. What it boils down to, really, she was more daddy's girl, shall we say? And when Kathleen came on the scene, she didn't like it. You with me? She wanted all my attention, you know, which she did have when she was younger, but when I got in with Kathleen, obviously I gave Kathleen a lot of attention which she needed because her husband was terrible to her - he never showed her any love or anything. Bernadette said to me her favourite record was 'Daddy's Home' - you know that one?

Cliff Richard?
That's the one. She was always playing that, she said. She never got on with Kathleen. One day, she just went off - completely out of site. I didn't know where she'd gone. She went off in a huff. She had a bee in her bonnet about

Kathleen, so she went off and she disappeared for twelve years.

How did you meet up again twelve years later?
All of a sudden, this photo appears in The Echo. A big photo of her, and she had two little ones with her and a caption saying, 'Come forward Ronald O'Connor' it said, 'you're a grandfather, Mr O'Connor, you're a grandfather twice over!'. Then it said about how she was looking for me, trying to trace me. 'I want to find my dad,' it said, 'I don't know where he is now, but I want to find him very much.' She couldn't remember where I lived in Cheltenham, you see? It was all over the paper. They had a photo of me which she must have kept, and they put that on there as well.

'You want to look in The Echo,' somebody told us, 'there's something about your daughter.' I got a copy and looked and there was the photo, a lovely picture, in colour, and a phone number for me to call.

That must have been a nice surprise.
I was amazed! I was so happy to see that photo, with the two little ones - the two boys Zack and Zen. It was like looking at Morgan all over again! I got in touch with her, of course, then we started going to see her. She got this house in Gloucester, two or three bedroom.

Did you get to know your grandsons?
Oh yes! I went round there all the time. I had a terrific rapport with the three boys. I mean, I gave them a lot of affection. Their dad, Andy, he didn't - he was very cold. He said to me once, well I didn't want them anyway. That's sums it up, dunnit, really? And I, I know what that's like because my dad never showed me affection and I tried to make it up, with them, what their dad wasn't giving them. We became very close with all the boys.

144

Do the boys take after you at all?
Well, they were interested in my music and my singing. Zack has obviously followed me for the voice because there was a show and they wanted to do a thing of Freddie Mercury's life, and he was picked for the main part, so obviously he must have a good voice. I wanted to go along and see it and all, but Bernadette said no - she made some excuse up or other. And nobody took any photos of it even.

That's a shame.
You were not allowed to take photos, apparently, because a lot of people were interfering with kids and all and they thought if you take a photo, you could use it on the internet or something. I don't know what it was about but there weren't any photos so all I know is he did this thing and he did well. Zack can definitely sing.

What about Zen?
I got him this little guitar - it was only a little child's guitar. He was about two or three then. I put it in his hand and he immediately put it the other way - he's a leftie, you see? That shows there's an interest, of course, so he takes after me in that way, I think.

When did you last see Bernadette and the boys?
I've not seen any of them for years. It's all because I didn't go to Liam's funeral. Bernadette has never forgiven me for that. I couldn't face it, I really couldn't. I was in too much of a state and the doctor said, 'You shouldn't drive in your condition.' But because I didn't go, Bernadette didn't want to see me again. Because of Bernadette being like this, of course, I've missed years with the boys, Morgan and Zen and Zack, which I can't get back. I regret it now - I should have gone to the funeral.

Chapter 18

Sean, Annette & Bridget

What do you remember about Sean when he was little?
Not a lot, really. He was a different kettle of fish altogether
than Bernadette. He wasn't a big child. A different build
altogether. He had very long arms, I do remember!

Like Mr. Tickle?
That's right - just like him, he was. They went through the
windows and up and around and everything!

How inconvenient.
It was! He takes after me for that. In the hospital, the things
he wore looked all wrong because his arms were so long.
And of course, he kept tickling the nurses and they didn't
like it!

What happened to Sean?
Like I said, Sean went to the same foster home as
Bernadette, but Chris Creswell didn't bother Sean; he was
only interested in the girls. I didn't see a lot of Sean, when
he was being fostered.

They were dreadful people, the ones fostering him. He was
always running me down, you know, saying, you know

why you're here? Because your father's no bloody good. Preaching to them, which is ironic, given what he was doing. Hypochrophal.

Hypochrophal?
You know - he was saying one thing and doing another thing. And the foster mother was a bitch. She had some relation who was a butcher, so they had liver all the time until they got sick to the back teeth of it. She was getting it cheap, see? Sean wasn't very happy there. He ran away several times and they kept bringing him back.

Did you get to see him?
No, they wouldn't let me come and see him. Except one time when he ran off, he eventually found his way to me and Kathleen. In a right state, he was. He'd been sleeping rough. He stank and his clothes were all horrible. I said, 'You can't go on like this.' So, we gave him a nice bath and everything and got his clothes nice and all. And we knew they'd be coming around, so we hid him.

You hid him?
Yes - and they didn't find him. We knew they'd be looking for him, you see? So, we hid him in this cupboard. It was very clever the way we did it because the drawers came out and you couldn't know there was anyone in there. The police came over because he was absent without leave or whatever you call it. He'd tried running before. He was about nine, ten, I 'spose. We hid him for a few days. We let him stay because we felt so sorry for him, the poor lad. Then we took him back.

What happened to Sean after that?
When he was old enough, he left his foster parents and got on with his life. He got a flat in Hester's Way. He's still there now, as far as I know. When I found out where he was living, I'd go up every so often to see him, and have meals

with him. It was alright, fine.

What does Sean do for a living?
He does decorating and all. He's a good hard worker. Very
good at painting and doing wallpaper and everything.

How did you and Sean get along?
Oh fine, good, yeah. I went over to his flat loads of times,
and he'd come up to us and he came to our marriage
blessing and everything. He was into Kung Fu - into it in a
big way, I mean - which is why I gave it a try. We
connected because of that. He had, in his flat, what they call
a wooden man, if you know what that is?

Is it like a man, but made of wood?
Sort of. It's made of wood and it's got things sticking out.

Hmmm.
And you go: bang, bang, bang, bang. You hit your arm
against each of the wooden things. It increases your speed
and all and your blocking. And he got really good at it. It's
Kung Fu - different from Karate. Karate is all smash, hit
smash; Kung Fun is more subtle, but it's very good for,
very effective against kicks. Sean got high up in it, and I
thought I'll have a go because I was interested so I joined
his club for a bit. The teacher there, he was great, and I did
quite well with that.

Did you practice with Sean?
Not really, no. He used to have the wooden man and I
didn't do that. I wanted to get one but they're quite dear. He
managed to get one second-hand.

Have you kept up with him since then?
Yes, yes, more or less. He got together with Debbie, that's
his wife. He had two lovely girls off her. But their marriage
didn't work out, unfortunately, but the girls kept in touch

with him, you know? I saw them back a few years -
beautiful looking girls. They look O'Connery - they don't
look like her, you know?

Are you still in touch with him?
No, I'm not. We've had a bit of a split up, I'm afraid. He
got in with this black woman and that was fine. I know her,
I met her, and she was a really nice lady. She was running
this home where Kathleen and I were living, and I got to
know here through that. She's a nice girl. I said to her, 'I'll
give you some guitar lessons' and she was interested, you
know? But! But! There's a big but! He's also had an
offspring off her, a girl or a boy, I don't know, and I don't
agree with him having a child off her.

What's the problem?
I just don't agree with that, you see? That's me, that's only
my opinion: I don't believe in mixing bloods. I want my
grandchildren to be the same as me, you know? Call me
racist of you like, but that's what I believe.

I can't say I agree with you.
That's just what I believe. And I saw the results when we
were living in Shipston. This girl got drunk, and dropped
her knickers, because that's what she did, and this black
guy had her and the result was this girl and she had so many
health problems - because of the bloods not mixing.

You believe that's why the baby had health problems?
It's like trying to put oil and water together. The oil comes
to the top, don't it? The black blood and the white blood
don't like each other. And she had all sorts of problems.
She had to have parts removed from her - inside, I mean.
She'll never be well; she's got major health problems and
they've told her it's because of mixing the bloods.

Who told her that?

The doctors told her. That's why the little girl was so ill.

Are you sure the doctors said this?
Yes, that's what I heard. It's the blood disease they get, because of the black blood. It's like a leukaemia. Sickle cell, that's it. She's had so many operations, this girl. Terrible. Poor girl. I mean, she's going to suffer now because of what her mum did. The mum was drink and let this guy have his way. He didn't want to know, after. And she's got all these major health
problems. She's suffering but she shouldn't be. The mum's fine but the girl's not. Sean's boy or girl is going to have the same problem, you know?

What about Meghan Markle?
What do you mean?

She seems fit and healthy.
Yeah, but she's not mixed race.

Yes, she is.
She can't be. The Royal Family wouldn't allow it!

We can look it up later - I'll show you.
I still don't believe it's right.

OK. OK. So, what happened when Sean and Debbie had the baby?
Well, Sean knows what I think, what my opinion is, so we haven't spoken since then. I told him, over the internet, an email, that Kathleen and I had split up but that's it.

So, you don't want to meet your grandchild?
Not really. I don't agree with it. I'm not really interested. That's just the way I am, the way I think of it.

Do you know what happened to Annette and Bridget?

150

Annette - she was very lucky, not like some of the others. She was adopted by an Irish couple who were really good, and they were very, very rich. They had this lovely house up in the Hamptons, which is a very posh area in Cheltenham. They adopted her. They didn't have any other kids. And they gave her a top education and everything and consequently she became a barrister. She's done well for herself. But I didn't get to see her.

Not even a chance encounter in Cheltenham?
No. Well, I'm not sure, actually. I was in Cheltenham, you see, about a year ago, and I think I saw her. I think it was her and I should have gone over, but I wasn't sure. If I go over to her and it's not her, I'm going to look like a right idiot, you know? But I think it might have been her because she said something to this little girl. About five, a beautiful little girl with lovely ringlets and all - the sort of child she would produce. And this little girl looked around at me because Annette must have said something to her. It might have been her - I don't know. And you've got to be so careful, you can't just go up to somebody.

Have you tried to trace her?
I know someone with a friend in social services and they might be able to trace her, wherever she is. Also, when Steve comes, that's the one that's doing the free computer course - he's been really good but it's the last time he's coming, next week, so I'm going to ask him if he'd put something on there for Annette. To say I'm looking for her and that.

And Bridget?
The one who adopted Bridget, it turns out, she was a lesbian. So, you can draw your own conclusions about that.

What are your conclusions?
Well, she was a big lez and obviously that probably

affected Bridget. I don't know whether it did or not but bound to, init? Her job: she was the Brown Owl for, erm, Scouts. Girl Guides. The one that's in charge. I didn't see Bridget when she was little, but I saw her a few year ago. I know she is living in Cheltenham, but I don't know where.

Did you have any more children with Jane?
The last two that we had were Ronald and then then Liam. The trouble is, they work on a principle of what they call the 'lemon' principle.

What's the lemon principle?
In other words, if one jumps off the cliff, they all jump off. That's how they think. What are you laughing about?

Nothing, sorry - carry on.
Well, because of the others being in care, they started on about Liam and about Ronald. Liam eventually went to a foster home. Ronald - I was looking after him because Jane was off on her trips.

Chapter 19

Ronald

How long did Ronald stay with you?
Not long enough, nowhere near long enough as far as I'm
concerned. The social worker said to me, about Ronald, he
was not even two, she said, 'You've got a lot on your plate
at the moment, why don't I take him for a bit now?' Until
you and your wife get sorted out.

That sounds reasonable to me.
Yes, but what she didn't tell me is that she'd already
planned it - she was very devious - she'd already got onto
these foster parents. I should have said no but I didn't. And
Ronald was, of course, he was absolutely beautiful looking.
Perfect, he was. I'm not just saying it, he was a beautiful
looking boy.

What did he look like?
Lovely white hair, you know? They thought he was an
albino he was so fair. And of course, they saw something
they couldn't produce, I suppose. Next thing is she says he's
up for adoption.I said, 'But you never said that to me!' She
had it all planned, I know she did. Back then, the social
workers were getting a dab in the fist from the foster
parents.

That's a bribe, right?
Yeah - for getting it arranged and all. No doubt, that's what
happened. I should have said to her no, I'm going to look
after him, which I regret but I trusted her, you see, that's the
trouble. I was quite capable of looking after him and I loved
him, obviously, like the others. I deeply regret it.

So, Ronald was adopted?
Yes, he was. Bernadette was very close with Ronald. She
was like his mother - you know what I mean? And when
they split them up, when Bernadette went into care, that
affected Ronald really badly. They'd been so close.

What was his adoptive family like?
The parents were really good. Ronald was very happy there.
But. And here's the big but. When he was twelve - that
would be in the mid '80s, I think - a friend of the foster
father raped him. Ronald told us - not at the time, much
later. I don't know whether it happened, or whether he
made it up or what, I don't know, but I can't see him
making that up. All I know is, it was all hushed up anyway.
The police weren't involved or nothing. But it affected him,
obviously. I only found out after he told me when we
eventually made contact with him. By the time we came on
the scene, the damage was done, I'm afraid.

How did it affect him?
After that, he started going odd in the head. He was hurting
himself. And later, a friend of ours was running this home -
she was taking people in that she found in the streets - she'd
actually found him in a box. Out in the street. She took him
in, and she felt really sorry for him and she managed to find
out who he was. She knew because of his lovely long hair,
lovely ringlets. He was well onto the drugs by then and he
was cutting himself, of course, as well.

What happened when Ronald left the foster home?
He had this little flat with this older woman. He wasn't
interested in young girls. She was like a mother figure, I
suppose - which he'd never had, obviously, with Jane. She
looked after him and all, but he ended up taking an
overdose, accidentally. He gave it up for a few months - got
clean - but this bloke came to where he was living and
persuaded him to go and have a what d-you call it. And
Ronald got sick, with the drugs, and the chap, instead of
him trying to help Ronald, he legged it. He choked on the
thing, you know? He was twenty-four, twenty-five, that's
all.

That's tragic.
I get upset still thinking about it. That day, by sheer luck, or
bad luck I should say, instead of his woman friend going to
the door, Ronald opened the door to him, this low life. 'I
can't,' he said, 'I don't have any money.' 'Don't worry, I'll
treat you,' he said. He'd gone several months without taking
anything, so his heart went, I suppose. I had to go and see
him - it was terrible. In the hospital. In this room, I don't
know what you call it.

I'm sorry.
I can still see it. I wish I couldn't, but I do. The foster
parents had a guilt complex, of course. They paid thousands
of pounds for the funeral. Well, it's the least they could do,
in't it?

What was Ronald like as a person?
He was lovely. About 6' 3". Took after his mum for the
hair. She had all ringlets, lovely long hair. He lived in a
time warp. He was in the sixties; everything was to do with
the sixties. That's what he was like. He wasn't interested in
the present. All to do with The Who and all those groups.
The music, the way they used to dress. He used to say, I'm a
free spirit. I still feel terrible about the fact that I let her take

him. I trusted her. She said he'd only be gone for a month or two.

Chapter 20

Liam

You said that Liam went to a foster home before Ronald?
He was staying with foster parents, which I didn't like. I
was never asked to come and meet him there, but I was
allowed to have him once a week. Then I noticed, when he
was having a bath, he had some bruising on him. On his
arms. I said to him, 'Where did you get that bruise?' But he
wouldn't tell me. And I kept onto him: where did you get
that bruising from? Oh, he said, 'It's the spoon.' His foster
mum was hitting him with this spoon or something, a
wooden spoon. The foster mother was laying into him. I
went ballistic. I wasn't having it, so I complained to the
social worker. We'll he went to them and they said, 'Mr
O'Connor is just a troublemaker.' They didn't like it. Next
thing is, they said they don't want me to have any more
access to him. He was eight then. I had access every
Saturday morning and I treasured that. It was a way of
seeing him and I used to give him a nice dinner and things.
I tried to bond with him, I 'spose. So, this was the last time,
the last Saturday I was going to see him. Well, I thought,
I'm not gonna not see him the rest of my life. I thought, I
can't accept that. I need to do something.

So, what did you do?

Well, I did something desperate. Stupid, really. It's a case of my heart ruling my head, I'm afraid. I just left the house as it was - the lovely house we had - put him in a pushchair and went and took him over to Germany.

You mean you kidnapped him?
It's not kidnap, if he's your own son!

Technically it is.
Well, there was no way I was letting him go back to that woman.

Why did you choose Germany?
You were able to get passports then, no problem - visitors' passports for Germany. And I'd lived in Germany, and I could speak the language. So we went over there and stayed in this hotel.

How did Liam take it?
He was worried sick, poor lad thanks to his foster mum. She'd told him, you see, if he ever takes you, he'll take you over to Northern Island and you'll get shot. Consequently, when I took him over to Germany, he was in such as state. He was shitting himself. Literally shitting himself, I mean. I said, 'This is not Ireland, this is Germany.' But it didn't make any difference. The chap that run the hotel was a real child lover, he said, 'Don't worry about that!' He'd made a mess everywhere and I'd got the sheets. 'Don't worry,' he said, 'the boy's nerves are in state, that's all. Bless him.'

What did you do for money?
I got myself a job there. Very good job with this bloke. He owned all these flats. In Munich, this was. I was doing really well there, and everything was fine. Liam was picking up the language, of course they do. Went to school and picked up the German language and all. It was all lovely.

158

What made you come back?
The trouble was, I also went with this girl, Barbara. This
was after Jane finally went off for good. She was a chopsy
bitch, Barbara was. I shouldn't have gone with her. When
we were over there, she wanted me all to herself, basically,
and she didn't want to know about Liam. Next thing I
know, she phoned her mum and told her where we were
and everything. So, they found out where we were living
and that was it. Mucked it all up. The social worker came
over to Germany and promised me that there was no way
they would let him go back to the same foster parents. What
did they do? Straight back to the same ones.

Do you regret taking him?
No, I don't! What else could I have done? I didn't want to
lose him. He was my last one. What I should have done -
and it's easy, again, to think back, in't it? - I shouldn't have
gone to Germany, I should have taken him to Ireland. They
never would have got him back, then. Me being an Irish
subject and him, obviously my son - the Irish are very loyal
to their own. By going to Germany, they were able to
extradite him.

What happened to you when you got back?
I was arrested when I got back in England. For taking my
own child. The police took me back, in their car, to
Cheltenham and I was supposed to appear in court, or
something, but I didn't. They didn't take it further. I don't
think they wanted to because they knew they were in the
wrong, probably. I don't know. Of course, I'd lost my home
because I walked out. So, I was in bed and breakfast for
quite a while.

Did you try to see Liam again?
Well, I couldn't, could I? I wasn't allowed. But I got on to
my solicitor, because I was not happy about what had

159

happened. There was no right of appeal, then. If they took a kid, you couldn't appeal against them. I said, 'I want to go to Strasbourg, the human rights court.' Nobody had ever been to Strasbourg. My solicitor said, 'There's no chance of you getting there - nobody's ever gone there,' and I said, 'Well, I'm determined, I am going to go.' I stuck to my guns. It meant having to go through different courts first, but eventually I got there.

Was Jane involved?
No, she wasn't interested. She had the same chance to appear in court - two hundred pound a day, plus her plane fare to Strasbourg - and she didn't bother. Typical her, right? Didn't want to know. So, I ended up in the court with all these judges, twelve judges, on my own. I was going there because there was nothing you could do before - they could take your children and that's it. I had that changed, by going there.

So, the case was successful?
Oh yeah. I got about five thousand compensation, or something like that. And it changed the law! It took five years in all. The solicitor took us to this place, right, and he said, 'You see that room in there?' I said, 'Yeah.' 'That room is full,' he said, 'of Mr. O'Connor.'

Well, you must have lost weight since then.
Very funny! 'That's been built over the years,' he said, 'as you've been fighting.' All the paperwork - it was piled up. And boxes: O'Connor, O'Connor, O'Connor, O'Connor. 'If you don't think you've done enough,' he said, 'have a look at that lot!' I'd been a thorn in their side, I'm afraid! But a good thorn, I think.

Did the case get much publicity?
Quite a lot, yeah. Kathleen and I were together by then, so she was there when the phone kept ringing all the time - all

160

these reporters and all. It was all over the papers. I've got all the papers kept, and all. It's all in a brown envelope. They had a cartoon, in there, as well, will us all saying, 'We've been to Strasbourg!' 'Cos obviously, these other couples heard about it, but I'm the one that instigated it. They climbed on the bandwagon and I thought, why not? This other woman, I remember, she had two or three children taken and she couldn't cope because she was on the drink, which is fine, but instead of trying to help her and get her to AA and all, they just took the kids. I think she was thinking of committing suicide - it affected her very badly. But you can't win - they were funny with me because I didn't drink!

Really?
They said I was anti-social.

Because of you not drinking?
Yes! You see what I'm saying? There were all these people that had a raw deal with social services - they joined the bandwagon - but my name's down in the record. I took the United Kingdom government to court! I thought, I don't see why I should suffer because my wife has got a drink problem, which she had - and she's a liar as well: she made a statement which is a pack of lies - so I decided, that's it - I need to do something about it. I wanted it so that people like me have the right of appeal and the judges agreed with me.

But despite the success of the court case, Liam stayed with his foster parents?
They all did. I'd won the right to appeal but the trouble was I couldn't afford a barrister.My solicitor said that if I had a barrister, which I didn't have, that I'd have had the children back next week. He'd have taken them to pieces, because there was no evidence. They didn't find anything wrong with the kids, but there was nothing I could do because I didn't have the money for a barrister.

What happened to Liam?
He was unlucky, Liam was, because it was a while before
he was adopted. Before that, you see, they got a lot of extra
money. They got this, that and the other, a free car, all
because of the fostering. But as soon as the adoption is
done, it all stops. Well, he was having a lovely time with
his foster parents. They were going off to this place on
holiday, then off to another place. He'd got accustomed to a
certain lifestyle, you know? But, as soon as they adopted
him, it all stopped. No money from the social services
anymore. Well then, he thought to himself what's going on
here? I've been used to this lifestyle and now, all of a
sudden, it's all changing.

How did it affect him?
He was used to the highlife when he was young but after he
got adopted and also when left home, he wanted the same
things, but he couldn't afford them. He started buying
things and not paying for them. Getting into debt. He was
living up in Birmingham, in a flat up there and I went to see
him a few times. This is when I managed to make contact
with him. He had this huge, big telly - he wouldn't tell me
where he'd got it from. Then he showed up with this
camera, which is about two grand's worth. Well, I thought,
how's he going to afford that, you know? He had a good job
in computers: an I.T. thing. So, a good brain, clever. But he
still got into debt. And he was gambling, big time, that was
another problem - making it worse. He was up to his eyes in
debt. Bernadette said he owed somebody thousands. And he
was doing drugs, expensive drugs. Sean told me one time
Liam went around to his place with this girlfriend of his and
they were rolling the thing up, you know, the notes? And
sniffing it all up their nose, using the notes. They said to
Sean, 'Would you like one' and he said, 'No, I've got work
to go to in the morning, I'm not doing it.'

Was he on his own?
No, he was with this girl. Her parents didn't like him because he was up to gambling and drugs and all sorts of stuff. She got pregnant and they had this little boy, my grandson, who I'll probably never see, I suppose. He'd be about five… maybe ten, by now. I'm not sure.

Did he manage to get out of debt?
Well, it all came crashing down, I'm afraid. He had, of course, these debt collectors after him. They come after you and if you don't pay 'em they break your legs. They kept coming to me and I wouldn't tell them where he lived. The things - the birds - were starting to hover, shall we say? I borrowed him a few hundred pound, but I couldn't afford much more. I don't know how much debt he was in, but I think he was in much more debt than he made out. I wish he'd of come to me - I'd have sorted something out. I could of taken him to a debt place to pay his debts off and I'd have got them off his back. 'Cos I was then very heavily into martial arts and I wouldn't have put up with their messing. I'd have sorted them out. But he didn't tell me.

So, what happened?
He took his own life.

When was the last time you saw him?
He was up Bernadette's. I gave him a big hug. Little did I know that was the last time I was going to see him. I'd love to see his son, if I could. I bet he looks just like Liam. I've got a very strong strain in me, you know? It takes over, you know what I mean?

Strong genes?
Stronger than denim, my genes are! Bernadette is the same: all the kids look like her. I bet Liam's little boy looks like me.

How did you hear about Liam's death?
Well, apparently, he never got to work, and they wondered
what was going on. The police kicked the door in, and they
found him with a needle in his arm. Poor lad. Terrible. It all
started, really, it all boils down to Jane making that
statement. She withdrew it but it was too late. All the cogs
had started moving. They were looking at a chance to get
their own back on me anyway, because I took her out of
their care. They said it at the time - we've got long
memories.

*So, you had to say goodbye to another one of your
children?*
Such a waste of life. I didn't go to the funeral. I should have
done. I regret it, but I didn't. It was a cremation which I
don't agree with. My religion doesn't believe in it. It's a
pagan thing, that's why. They're saying, in other words,
there's nothing, you know, that you're just nothing. They
don't say about there being an afterlife or nothing.

You should tell this to Pope Francis!
What's that?

He has said it's OK for Catholics to be cremated.
Where did you hear that?

On the news, a little while ago.
Well, I don't think it's right. Anyway, they did a cremation,
the foster parents did, because it was the cheapest funeral
they could buy. They couldn't care less about Liam. He
played them up, so that was it. They were only his foster
parents so they thought, why should I pay for it? After all
that trouble - taking him up to Germany - I couldn't face
going to see him just turned to ashes like that. I just couldn't
do it.

Where was the funeral?

It was where he lived, up in Birmingham. There was no way I could drive all the way to Birmingham. I was on these tablets off the doctor - I mean very strong tablets - to try and come to terms with Liam dying, you know?The doctor said, 'It's illegal for you to drive when you're on these tablets.' But Bernadette was not happy about it. She came to see me and Kathleen and she said, 'I don't really want to go to Liam's funeral,' she said, 'I'm really not interested' this was her words by the way 'but I'm going anyway, and you should too. I'm going because of the boys,' she said, 'I want them to come.' And Emily came too so there was no room in the car for me. Now what she could have done, if she'd wanted to, she could have said to Emily, 'Well, he's nothing to do with you, really,' and let me go in her place in the car. If she said that, I'd have gone.

But you hate funerals. Would you really have gone?
I'm not sure. Maybe I wouldn't of gone, because, well, this is the boy I took over to Germany and gave my home up for and now she's trying to make out I didn't care about him, which is a load of rubbish. I shouldn't
have to go to his funeral to prove to her that I loved him! But I do regret not going.

How did Bernadette react to you not going to the funeral?
Not well, I'm afraid. Afterwards she came back and she wrote this horrible letter to me. 'I don't want to know you anymore,' she said, 'you're not my father anymore, don't try to contact me or the children ever again et cetera, et cetera'. A stinking letter - really nasty it was.

Why was she suddenly so angry with you?
It was just because I didn't go to the funeral.

Really?
That's Bernadette for you. She has a lot of troubles. I think being in that foster home affected her - bound to of done.

165

She tends to make stuff up. She tells porky pies, I'm afraid. You really don't want to meet her.

Did you try to contact her?
I tried to talk to her loads of times. I rang her number and one of the boys, Zak, I think, picked the phone. Oooh, it's grandad, it's grandad! He was all excited, which he would be, because he knew me, and the next thing - bam! She slammed the phone down. And that was it. She changed the number. That was years ago, now. I haven't seen them since.

That's sad.
I hope I'll see them again one day.

Let's hope.
Well, she came back to me after twelve years before so it could happen again.

Let's call it a day there. You've come up with plenty more material for me to work on.
How's the book coming along?

Pretty well, I think. It's just hard getting everything in the right order.
Well, I don't remember when things happened, I'm afraid.

That's how the memory works, I guess.
But at least it is working. Let me get your coats for you.

Thanks.
Make sure you don't catch that virus. No shaking hands - use the elbow thing or whatever.

Namaste?
Bless you. Ha, ha! And don't forget to sneeze into you elbow.

OK, OK, I'll be careful.
So will I. See you in a couple of days?

Yeah - I'll let you know.
OK. Bye for now.

Bye Kevin.
Bye.

Chapter 21

Kathleen

Hello Kevin!
Hello. Come in. Put your coat on the hook. That's right.
What about this virus then?

It's all over the news.
I know!

Lots of countries are taking measures.
Closing schools and pubs and all that. In Ireland even!

That's going to hit them hard.
Imagine them having no Guinness. For weeks!

It'll probably do them some good.
I 'spose it will. Come and sit down. I'll do us some tea in a
minute.

You OK to get started?
Yup.

*So, you've mentioned Kathleen many, many times - she
must have become an important part of your life?*

She's the love of my life!

When did you meet her?
It was quite soon after I came back from Munich with
Liam. I was in bed and breakfast for a while, but I got on to
this councillor and she was really, really good. I told her
about everything that had happened and all. She put a lot of
pressure on and eventually, she got me a place in
Cheltenham, in Pittville, which is a good area. Irving
House, called after the councillor, Mr. Irving. A whole
block of flats. Only a bedsit but it was really nice.

Were you single by then?
Yes, I was. Jane was long gone and Barbara, well, she was
a nuisance to say the least. This was at the start of the
eighties. I was on my own, but then I met Kathleen. I had
started going to the Robins. It's a football club, but they
also do the country and western shows there. If you didn't
get there by half seven, you wouldn't get in, it was so
popular. They used to have a shoot-out with the guns, not
real guns, and there was a dance. They had one every week.
That's where I met Kathleen. She was with her husband,
but he wasn't bothering with her. And she was looking over
at me a lot. I smoked a pipe then, of course, and she thought
I was very wealthy, which I wasn't, but that's neither here
nor there.

Did you approach her?
Yes, but I did the right way. I said to her husband Bill, 'Do
you mind if I dance with your missus?' He said, 'You can
dance with her all you like, for all I care.' I thought: that's
very nice. I felt a bit sorry for her, really. I put my arm
around her, and she liked the affection, you know? She
looked lovely. She had all the gear on, stockings and all this
business - dressed up in the country and western. She
looked after herself, you know?

169

You mean you fancied her?
Yes, of course I fancied her! And we got on really well. She was very fond of the booze, then, probably because she was unhappy. Anyway, I left before she left. I got back to my flat and I thought, it's not on - she's a married woman and I respected that. And she's got this daughter: Donna she's called. I didn't want to break their marriage up. So, I didn't think any more of it.

When did you see her again?
Well, I was in town the next day and I heard someone shouting, 'Kevin!'. I couldn't hear who it was, and it was her. She was in her own clothes. I didn't recognise her, you see? Obviously, the night before she was all dressed up. I didn't recognise her, but she saw me, and she saw the way I was walking, a bit like John Wayne, she said, and something flipped, apparently.

John Wayne, the cowboy actor? Really?
'Get off your horse and drink your milk!'

You know he never actually said that, don't you?
Didn't he?

No. Why would cowboys drink milk?
Because it's good for their teeth?

Fair point. You were saying about meeting Kathleen again?
Oh, yeah. We really got on, you know? And as it happened, I had what they call a free ticket to the country show. If you win this thing, you get a free ticket for the following week. So, I let her come on my ticket. And we danced and it was really lovely, so I whispered her my phone number. But I thought, there's no way she'd going to remember that because she was really sozzled when we left the club.

But she did remember, didn't she?

170

Stop ruining the story! Yes, she did. The next day, the phone rang. She said she couldn't find exactly where I was, so she phoned from a phone box. It was only up the road from where I was, so I told her it's flat thirteen, and it's in Irving House. She managed to find it and she came up there, to my bedsit and I showed her around the place. Not much to see, really, but that was it. That was what we had.

Did she have any doubts?
Kathleen's friends tried to talk her out of it, you know? They said, 'What are you doing?' She had her own family after all. As well as Donna, she's got three boys, all older than Donna. One was Nick, he's the oldest. Then there's Mark and then Lee, the youngest. So, I said to her, 'I'll tell you what we'll do,' I said, 'why don't we leave it for a bit and see how you feel? Just for a month,' I said, 'don't contact me, and I won't contact you.' And she agreed. She was working at an old people's home as a cook, head cook, and after a week or so she was very unhappy. She missed me, you know, and they said to her, the people there, 'For god's sake, cheer up, go and bloody get onto him,' they said. So, she did all the running, not me. She phoned me up and she said, 'I want to see you.' but I said, 'I told you, wait for a bit, you know, because you're married, and all.' 'Oh, I don't care about that.' she said. Some of her friends didn't like it but she'd made up her mind, and that was it, really.

Did she move in with you?
After a while, she did. I was living in Irving House, second floor up. It was a bedsit, basically, but it was really nice. It had a cooker and a kitchen, well, only a little kitchenette. She was living in another place with her husband, and Donna, her daughter. But she said to me, she found happiness and peace with me, in the bedsit, that she couldn't find in her own home, even though she had a four-bedroom house.

171

How did things develop from there?
She came to the bedsit more and more. And she was staying later, and later, and later and one day she said, 'I'm not going back.' She didn't stay permanent, but she didn't go back that night. Then she went back to her house and he didn't even notice she wasn't there. Show's what he was like. Eventually she moved in with me.

It sounds like you were happy there.
We were happy. We were in love and it felt right, you know? It was a tiny bedsit, but it felt good and we liked it there. We never should have left there but we had to.

Why?
We got fed up there because there was this chap, underneath me. He was a drunk and he kept coming up all the time to see me. And, of course, when Kathleen moved in, he couldn't come up anymore and he started making trouble. He was getting drunk and shouting and all that. And he went for me, he tried to - which he shouldn't have - because I was very good at martial arts by then. We got into a fight. I got hold of him and gave him a good smack. That's neither here nor there, but he got what he deserved.

But why did you have to leave?
We were fed up with it, really. And the housing said we've got a lovely place for you to go to. Lovely place my bum! It was a basement. Biggest mistake we ever made. We should have stayed where we were. What they didn't say was about the damp. Riddled with damp, it was. Virtually riddled. It was dreadful. I had some lovely boots: covered in mould. They went green. Everything went green from the mould. It just ruined loads of our stuff. Old photos and that, things we could never replace.

But you eventually got out?
Yes, but we made another fatal mistake after that.

What did you do?
We decided to go to Munich.

Munich again?
Well, I knew Munich well, didn't I? And it's in Germany, which I love. And I had some money in the bank: the five thousand they awarded me in Strasbourg.

What could possibly go wrong?
Unfortunately, things did go wrong. We got in with this woman called Frau Doll, you see. She got us involved, which was fatal, into buying this house over there, which we were thinking of turning into a bed and breakfast. It would have been an investment. This was the mid-eighties - everyone was buying houses and making lot of money from. But the trouble was, it was a fiddle because we had a resident there who we couldn't get rid of. I think she saw us coming. Kathleen said to this woman, 'I've got some money to come.' And her eyes lit up, Frau Doll's, because she thought, great, we've got a right pair here. I've got my five grand and she's going to get another ten or fifteen which were the proceeds from half the house in Rosehill Street. We signed things and everything but then it all went belly up.

What was the problem?
We'd signed everything, right, but then we realised this chap was a resident so we couldn't throw him out. We couldn't turn it into a bed and breakfast, so we tried to back out.

But you'd already signed the contracts?
Yes, but we didn't know about the resident. Also, we didn't have the money after all. Kathleen didn't get her half of the money. He, Kathleen's husband that is, wasn't happy about it, was he? So, he appealed against it and the judge, excuse

173

my language, was an Irish hater, and he said no because their daughter was living there still. In fact, she wasn't living there at all, but her husband used that. The judge wouldn't grant Kathleen half the house even though she'd been the one that got the mortgage! I went to my solicitor and he said, 'I advise you,' he said, 'get out, now, otherwise you're going to be in real trouble.'

You mean, get out of the contract?
No - get out of the country! He advised us: get out while you can. We'd signed all the papers and everything, are you with me? But we didn't want the place and we didn't have the money. They would have had us, big time - the German authorities. We had to leave the country. But, the trouble was, we couldn't get out because we were being watched.

By the police?
Yes. The authorities. The people living in the same place as us had informed them. I know it sounds ridiculous but that's the way it was. They knew we were trying to leave. They were watching the house, so Kathleen and I couldn't go together. If they saw us with the cases and stuff, they'd have us. That's how bad it was. So, what we did - we came up with a plan. Kathleen was to go on ahead. Go back on her own. She left very early in the morning, when it was dark because of them watching us. She came back to Cheltenham and found a little bed and breakfast. Then, I came back, very early in the morning, same as Kathleen did.

You were outlaws!
I know, like Bonnie and Clyde.

Did you and Kathleen get back together?
Of course. We found another flat, and that was in Cheltenham again, I think. We stayed there for a while but what we really wanted was our own house, you know?

Somewhere special, for me and Kathleen. And we managed to get jobs, so we could afford it.

What kinds of work did you do?
I worked as a chef, with an agency, and Kathleen got this job in an old people's home. That's how we got this chance of a house. Kathleen met this old lady who owned this house in Whaddon Road. She said to Kathleen, because we were looking for a place, 'If you want the house, I'll give you a special price.' It was down at sixty-eight grand but, at that time there was a big recession, a very bad recession, and she said you can have it for a special price because she'd got to like Kathleen very much. Kathleen didn't only cook but she looked after the people - that's the way she is. So, we got this place at a bargain price. I think we got it for forty-two grand. Edwardian house. We were there for a while, a good few years, yeah. It was lovely.

Did you and Kathleen get married?
Yes, we did. We got married in 1988. It was in the summer. Could have been August maybe? I'm not sure.

How did you propose?
I said I was in love with her and I wanted her to be my wife. And that was it. I didn't have any reservations about it. I knew it was the right thing, you know? With the other one, Jane, I did have reservations. There was something in my head saying, don't do it, don't do it! And, oh boy, weren't they right? But with Kathleen, I was sure. No doubt in my mind at all.

What do you remember about your wedding day?
It was really good. One of Kathleen's relations, he videoed it for us. It was only on for a few minutes - I wish he'd done it longer, really. Her dad was there. He was a right sod. He didn't like Kathleen getting in with me, but he didn't like Kathleen getting in with anybody! Miserable git, he was.

175

Horrible man. He didn't understand someone like me: someone who doesn't drink. As far as he was concerned you weren't normal if you didn't drink. He was very fond of the booze. He wouldn't just have the beer, he'd have whiskies in it as well - what they call chasers. But anyway, he came to the wedding.

Who else was there?
Well, when we signed the papers at the church and all, the people that worked with Kathleen, they were there and that was nice. Kathleen's son Mark was there. He's a bit of a character, he was. He was dressed in dark glasses. Sean was there, my son. And Liam was still alive then. They all had these dark glasses. They looked like mafia! Bernadette was there. It was a lovely day, really.

Did you go on honeymoon?
I think we did, eventually, but not straight away. We went to Italy, or somewhere like that. We had several holidays which she never had when she was with her husband, you know? Italy was her favourite. We went there a few times, back to the same place. A very popular place with the tourists and all - can't remember what it's called. All by coach. And the boat, of course. We love the Italian food as well. The pizzas and things. They know how to make the pizza over there!

It sounds like you and Kathleen were happy in Whaddon Road?
We had some good times there. We were both working, making money, getting on fine, and we loved it there. But the mortgage started to get too high. It got to seventeen-point APR. You can imagine what it was like. Very expensive, you know? So, no more holidays, nothing like that, because we didn't have that kind of money anymore because the mortgage was so high. But my wages paid for the mortgage and her wages paid for the food and all, so we

were getting along fine. But everything changed when Kathleen had her accident.

Chapter 22

Kathleen's Accident

Tell me about the accident.
She was on her way up to work on her bike and this chap, a
taxi driver, he was parked outside McDonalds. The trouble
was, he didn't bother looking in his mirror. He opened the
door and she went smack into him. Over the handlebars.

Ouch.
They called an ambulance, of course, but the thing is, she
didn't realise how serious it was. She thought she'd carry
on to work, but the ambulance person said, 'No way!' I
only heard about it when she came back later. She said
about what happened and we went to see the doctor and he
examined her. Eventually, it turned out she'd damaged her
spine.

How did the accident affect Kathleen?
It really affected her. She lost her job.They said you've got
to go because you can't do the things you used to be able to
do - lifting these big plates and pans and so on. And we
went to see the doctor and he said, 'No, this is not on,
you'll have to look after her.' So, I had to pack my job. She
got worse and worse. When she'd have a shower, I'd wash
her back. I'd help her get dressed. I became her official full-

time carer. She also suffered from other things that weren't caused by the accident. OPCD which is problems with the lungs and she's a bad asthmatic anyway. And she had arthritis.

Did you sue the man who did it?
Ah, you see then - that's twenty year ago - you didn't have what you've got now: no win no fee. If it had of been, we'd have got more. We did take him to court, but the solicitor was useless; she didn't want to know. We had witnesses - it was entirely his fault - but we only got five grand out of it and by the time she'd taken her lot and all, solicitor's fees I mean, there was nothing. And, of course, the man came out of court grinning from ear to ear because he knew he'd got away with it. But it changed our life. That bloke in the car doing that, by him not looking in that mirror, it virtually changed our life. It really changed our life. And that's two incomes we lost so then we couldn't carry on with the mortgage.

How did you cope?
We sold that house and made a profit on it and we got another one, a smaller one, in Cheltenham up the road from there. What the woman didn't tell us - she was very crafty - there was a problem with the boiler and that cost us thousands. When we went there the heat was on all the time. The reason was because the boiler was going to pack up. She knew if she switched it off, it wouldn't come back on. We should have got British Gas to check the boiler and we could have knocked thousands off what we paid her. She was a crook, virtually.

Did the accident affect your relationship?
No, we got on fine with each other. We had ups and downs like everybody does, you know? I was looking after her. Washed her, dressed her, did everything, really, for her. I didn't begrudge it because I loved her.

Did you ever worry that she was getting seriously ill?
Oh yes. But funnily enough, nothing to do with the accident. A few years later, she had this heart attack. That was frightening, very frightening. We were going into town to this butcher's I always used to go to - they did really good stuff - in Cheltenham High Street. We walked up there but by the time we got there she was gasping for breath. He gave her some water and I said, 'That's not right.' 'Oh, well, it's only my asthma,' she said, but it wasn't her asthma causing this, it was her heart. Eventually, I said, 'Look' - she didn't want to do it – 'I'm making an appointment with the doctor.' 'But I don't want to bother with them.' she said. I said, 'We're making an appointment!' I had to literally take her there, almost dragged her there because she didn't want to go. Just by sheer luck, one of the girls that works behind, in the doctors - the health centre there - she said, 'Hang on a minute, I don't like the look of this. Tell you what I'll do,' she said, 'I'm going off work soon but before I go, you come on in and we'll do an OCG on you.' So, she took Kathleen in and connected her to this thing. 'Oh,' she said, 'I'm not happy with this at all' - the wires and stuff - and I said, 'Well I'm not either because there's something wrong.' The tests said she needed to be careful, so we knew what to look out for. If I hadn't of taken her that day, she'd not be around now. I knew there was something wrong. I do get these feeling sometimes, and they're usually right.

Were you right on this occasion?
Yes, I was because a few days later, she got bad. I called the ambulance and they came over. They said, 'I don't want to worry you, Mr O'Connor, but your wife has had a miniature heart attack.' 'Oh no,' I said. They took her off to Bristol in the ambulance straight away. I couldn't go in with them, so I followed in my car. I was right sick, worried sick because I loved her. I did love her, and I still love her. They

180

did all these tests and everything. I thought I was going to lose her, I really did. I watched her there and they said what they were going to do. She was in there for days. I tried to go up as much as I could because I didn't want to leave her there on her own. It worked out fine in the end. What she had to have done, she had these stents put in. The arteries or the things that go to the heart had been blocked.

Is that a type of heart surgery?
Sort of but they don't open you; they do it through a vein. Her being out of breath was her heart saying to her I can't get enough blood, you know? The stents seemed to help. After that she was fine.

Without jobs, did you manage to keep paying the mortgage?
No, we didn't. He had to sell the house and we moved to a bungalow in Gloucester. We walked away with about forty grand. The trouble was, we had to declare it.

Declare it?
All of it - to the benefits office. Because we had all this money, they wouldn't help us, you see? No benefits. Our savings had to pay for everything because we couldn't work, what with Kathleen being ill and me looking after her.

I guess that's just how it works.
Yes, but we wanted to have something to show for it, you know, all the money from the house? It wasn't fair. Just because of that one bloke, parked outside McDonalds, didn't bother looking in his mirror, opened his door and then, at that moment, everything changed. We didn't want all those mortgage payments to come to nothing. So, we decided to get rid of all this money and buy things with it. We decided to get some things we needed.

Chapter 23

Gloucester

What did you spend your savings on?
I said to Kathleen what we'll do, I tell you what, I'll get a guitar, a thousand, and I'll get you the top of the range, which she wanted, sewing machine, another thousand pounds. This sewing machine did everything. It embroids, I mean it does its own embroidery and everything. I thought, why not? She's got to get something as well. And also, we put some money towards a car and a few bits and pieces for the bungalow. Then I bought Kathleen one of those moveable chairs - you know the chairs that people use, electric chairs?

Sounds lethal!
Not that! You know, the ones for old people to get about?

Mobility scooters?
Yes, yes! Why did the electrician refuse to fix the electric chair? He said, 'I'm not touching that, it's a death trap!'

That's a really dreadful joke.
I know! I've got loads more.

Later, maybe.

The trouble was, she couldn't get on with it, so I had to sell that. It was over three grand and he put the cheque in like that so I couldn't stop it, could I? We got about three hundred for it, so I lost big money on that.

How was your time living in Gloucester?

The people around there weren't good, I'm afraid. There was an Irish chap living next door and I said to him, being the way I am, I said 'You're always very welcome to come and have a cup of tea' or something like that and his remark to me was, 'I DON'T DO TEAS!' So rude, he was. He got quite nasty with me and after that. I wouldn't talk to him. Well, he stirred this other woman who was a right troublemaker, an out and out bitch, and eventually we weren't very popular around there. Not our doing. It was but because he stirred this other woman up.

Did you get on with anyone there?

There was one girl we got in with. She was really nice, and we got very friendly with her. I can't remember her name now. She was in her twenties I suppose. We felt sorry for her, originally. She was always outside the door, on her own and I said to Kathleen, 'We've got to do something about that, I feel sorry for that girl.' Kathleen said, 'I feel the same, why don't we invite her in?' She wouldn't come in at first - she obviously didn't trust anybody - but eventually we persuaded her to come in and we gave her a nice meal and she seemed to brighten up, you know? She was obviously suffering from very bad depression, the poor girl, so we let her into our home. We became friends with her, and we trusted her, of course, but that turned out to be a big mistake.

What happened?

Well, we trusted her, but we shouldn't have. She was a nice girl, but she was particularly good at flashing, if you know

what I mean? You know, flashing, showing everything
when she was in the house. She was coming over all the
time, skirts up around here. It was obvious what she was
trying to do. I think she was trying to get off with me, but
Kathleen had her weighed up. Anyway, we told her things,
private things, things that we shouldn't have, and it got
back to us. She'd been saying things behind our back. Even
though we were having her in with meals. We spoilt her.
We looked after her and were really good to her, you
know? She turned on us. Stabbed us in the back, virtually.

What kinds of things did you tell her?
All personal stuff, you know? We told her loads of things
only because we thought we could trust her. Things you
don't tell people normally, but we told her, I suppose,
because of the way she wormed her way in.

Why do you think she started telling other people?
I don't know. I think she became a bit jealous. I remember
this time when they were celebrating a thing around there,
about the housing, and Kathleen had designed the cake
especially. It was so many years since they'd opened this
place and we got on like that with the manager. He was a
terrific bloke and he couldn't get over the moon about how
Kathleen had done this special cake for them with all the
flowers and all. We took the cake over and this girl, the one
we trusted, got a bit jealous because, obviously, Kathleen
was getting the attention. She's an attention getter, this one,
as we found out. And she got steadily worse, you know,
and stirred the others up. It went from bad to worse and I
thought: we've got to get out of here.

Did you get to know any other neighbours?
There was also this older woman there who was very
elderly. She'd been left a big pension by her husband. She
was very well off, but we felt sorry for her being on her
own, so Kathleen started doing her meals on the weekends

184

just because we'd always have extra left over. I don't think she could believe it - how nice we were. Then Christmas came, the first Christmas there, and we said to her, 'How would you like to spend Christmas with us?' Well, she thought we were joking, I think. Anyway, she spent Christmas with us, and we spoilt her rotten - gave her everything. She had a fantastic time. This went on and in the new year I used to go up the road because she likes her whisky, so I got her a bottle every second day. I had to do the shopping for her and everything and Kathleen then started doing her meals in the middle of the week as well. Kathleen is a fantastic cook, always has been. And she was very grateful and everything, but she never offered us a penny. It was costing us quite a bit, but I thought, I don't mind.

It sounds like you were very kind to her.
We were kind to her, but she wasn't kind to us, it turns out. When it came to the crunch, we had to leave the flat quick. We had so long to get out - the council were a right funny lot. They gave us a deadline, so we had to get all our stuff together. We didn't get a removal van; we tried to do as much of it as we could. We took what we can in my car and said to the old woman we'd been giving the meals to and everything, 'Would you mind looking after some of our stuff over night?' 'Oh no, I couldn't do that.' she said. After what we'd done for her! Anyway, as a result of that we had to leave some stuff outside and, of course, when we come back to pick the rest up it had all been thieved. Loads of stuff were lost. She didn't like it because she knew we were leaving, and she wasn't going to get any more meals, that's what I think.

Had she heard the gossip?
Everyone did, I'm afraid.

It must have been serious, whatever they were saying about

you.
We should never have trusted her, that's all.

Chapter 24

Hester's Way

So, where did you go next?
After Gloucester? It was the millennial, around that time - I think we moved to another bungalow for a bit but soon after we moved to Hester's Way, back in Cheltenham. My son Sean lived just up the road from there. And Marie still lived there, which we didn't know until later. It was a big mistake, moving there.

What went wrong?
There was this chap I used to be with years ago. I had like a duo with him for a while. Not a duo really - he used to play the guitar and I'd sing. We did a few things together, but it wasn't much. Well, when he saw me, he said, 'Wooah! Ronald!'. I said, 'Oh, hello, how are you?' All excited, he was. This is twenty years after I'd been with him. He assumed, which he shouldn't have, that I was going to get back with him. He saw the dollar signs, shall we say, because he knew we used to make good money. I wouldn't go back with him anyway - I wanted a fresh start. And he had two dogs, two yappy dogs so I wouldn't be able to go up to his flat to rehearse, anyway. I'm allergic, you see, to dogs. Sharp he was called, by the way. His family are a right lot of gypsies, like. His mum was a bright spark, she

went with all the Americans during the war. She was a slapper, but that's neither here nor there. When the penny dropped with him that I wasn't going to go back with him he started turning nasty. And Marie knew him - from when he and I were together - and she started stirring it, spreading all these lies about me.

You said Sharp turned nasty?
He got our car wrecked. His brothers ruined it one night. Gypsies all together. They came there, very late, and smashed all the windscreens. It was a wreck. Thousands of pounds worth of damage done. Others there watched them do it and didn't bother getting the police or nothing. They were afraid of him, that's why.

Sharp was a violent man?
Violent? I should say. He's a horrible bloke, but he gets away with it. He attacked this Irish chap with a hammer. The chap, a lovely man, managed to close the door so, of course, he smashed all the door instead. It was like that movie. The one Jack Nicholson was in - The Shining.

Here's Johnny!
Here's Sharpy! It was just as scary, I can tell you.

Why did Sharp have it in for you?
It was because I wouldn't have anything to do with him.

He smashed your car because of that?
He was an Irish hater, Sharp was, you see? We stood up to him, and he didn't like it. There was this lady in the flats on the opposite side. A lovely, lovely lady. Sue, she was called. Me and Kathleen became very good friends with her. She was a really decent, posh lady. She shouldn't even be living there, really. She hated Sharp because he was making abuse to her, making sexual remarks to her, saying when you have a shower, call me and I'll do your back for

188

you, you know? Sharp started making her life hell. He thought he was irresistible to women, but he wasn't, and she couldn't stand him. He gives me the creeps, she said, 'I'd rather turn lesbian before I let him touch me,' she said. He went and smashed her balcony. She was just sitting there, reading her book, having a bit of peace, and he couldn't leave her alone. He went and broke all her things, all this stuff she had up there, pots and everything. He was a little git. He's evil, he's pure evil. Sue had a daughter and he started saying things to her when she was coming up the stairs. Innuendos, you know what I mean? I said, 'Call me if he ever tries anything.' because he knew I wasn't frightened of him.

Do you think Sharp heard what Marie was saying about you?
Yes, everyone did, I'm afraid - she was a right stirrer.

What had she been saying about you?
She was saying all sorts of crap. What was it? I'm a child molester - all sorts of rubbish

What?
It was horrible, really horrible. All lies, of course. We didn't know she was still living there, otherwise we wouldn't have gone there. Because of her, things went from bad to worse.

What happened?
I got this letter, a poison pen letter, and the things it said on there was disgusting, terrible - saying I'm a child molester. He'd written the letter, Sharp had. I know for a fact he did.

How do you know he'd written it?
Because I could tell. The stuff that was in it and also, we saw him later with some brown envelopes exactly the same. It was him alright. I wasn't happy about that, as you can

imagine. Then he came to the door of my flat. You had to press the thing, or you couldn't get in otherwise. He said, 'I wanted to talk.' Anyway, I shouldn't have, but let him in because he seemed alright, you know? So, he came up to the door and we were getting on alright. He was giving me all syrup and all, but as soon as I mentioned about the letter he had written - which I know he wrote, I'm sure of it - he changed then. He denied it, of course. Next thing is, he punched me there - right between the eyes. He took me on the hop.Of course, I stood there and let him, I don't think. That was a fatal thing to do. I said to him, 'You shouldn't have done that.' and, of course, I retaliated. I gave him a good pasting, which he deserved.

Was Kathleen in the flat?
Oh yeah. She phoned the police. I got him on the floor, and I laid into him because I had a lot of reason to. He said, 'I didn't do that to the car.' which I know he did. And he wrote that letter.

You were very angry with him?
Yes, of course I was! He was out cold, eventually, on the floor. And I was thinking about chucking him down the stairs to finish him off.

What are you saying?
I thought about it. But then I thought, mmm. If I had, he'd have died, you see?

Right.
And here was this other chap downstairs, outside another flat. Sharp's friend. He was high on this drug or something, maraguana you call it? Whacky backy. A complete fruitcake - he thought he was an Indian chief. He'd go around with all the feathers and go 'Oooooyyyyeeer' and I thought, oh god. And people say it doesn't do you any harm! Anyway, if this bloke hadn't been there, I was going

throw him down the stairs.

I see.
The other chap down the stairs would have seen me. He would have been a witness. So, I didn't bother.

Thank God.
Anyway, he didn't show himself for a week because of his injuries. Apparently, when he did show, he looked like a panda! He was very silly attacking me.

Did you get into trouble for the attack?
Not really. He attacked me, you see? Sharp told the police I attacked him, but they knew what he was like. But then he got on to the council and there was this one from the council, the housing one, she came up and was all on his side. They were backing him up, all the council, for some reason. It's because they were up his arse; they thought he was great. This councillor, she came up to me and I said, 'That's self-defence.' 'Oh no it's not', she said, 'you attacked him!' 'I said, 'Only because he attacked me.' She got really nasty with me and pointed her finger at me and said, 'It's not self-defence, I'm going to have you for that, I'll get you to court!' And I said, 'Go ahead!'

Did it go to court?
No, it didn't go to court because a new chap took over the council and he came to see us, and he sorted her out. He got her the sack. He knew that we were decent, and he knew what Sharp was like.

What happened to Sharp?
They built up this dossier on him: attacking the Irish chap, breaking our car and all and so many things that he'd done. But somehow, he got away with it. I think, reading between the lines, he was a police informer because when it went to court, they had so much on him, but he got off scot free.

191

Why do you think Marie said what she said about you?
I don't know why she say's anything. She's a nut case, that's what I know. By spreading around things that weren't true, it made our name mud. We couldn't stay in Hester's way after that.

Where did you go?
We had another bungalow for a while but the landlord there conned us. There was wallpaper where we had the shower, instead of tiles. Of course, the inevitable happened, water was going down, leaking as it does, down to the flat underneath. So, he blamed us for that. Any excuse, so he wouldn't give us back our deposit because, he said, you caused all this damage.

After that, we went to Shipston-on-Stour. Kathleen has a very good friend there called Margaret Williams. We went around and saw a bungalow and liked it there. We were there for nine or ten years. We loved it in Shipston.

OK, that's enough for today, I think.
OK. Will I see you again next week?

Yes. So long as this virus doesn't get any worse.
Yes, OK. Scary isn't it, this virus?

Well, people haven't been asked to stay at home like in Italy.
Not yet.

We'll see what the government is saying next week - it changes all the time.
OK. You will look after yourself, won't you?

I will. And let me know if you need anything.
I will, thanks. And I really appreciate what you're doing,

you know that?

I know.
See you soon. Mind how you go.

Bye.
Bye.

Chapter 25

Shipston-on-Stour

Hello Kevin.
Hello young man!

You're well, I hope?
I'm fine, I'm fine. Come on in. I'll get the kettle on. Come on through.

I'm not sure if I should have come.
Because of the virus?

Yes. People can still see each other for the time being but they've started saying that old people in particular should be careful.
But you're not ill, are you?

No, I'm fine. And I've not been in contact with anyone who's been ill.
Well, that's OK then.

Yes, but just to be on the safe side, let's sit a bit further apart.
OK, I'll move my chair.

And let's forget about the cup of tea, shall we?
Good thinking.

You ready to get started with the book?
Fire away!

You were saying, last time, that you moved from
Cheltenham to Shipston. When was that?
Let me think. It must have been two thousand and four or
five, I 'spose. We were there for about ten years, anyway.

And you said you liked living there?
Yes, we did. It was all the people, mainly. We met a lovely
couple there. Betty Early, unfortunately not with us
anymore, bless her, and her husband. He was mad about
country music and I used to often go in with my guitar and
sing to him. Lovely man. I really got to love him. He died
and Betty wasn't the same after. They were so close.

How did you get to know the Earlys?
I did a lot of shows there, in Shipston. Variety shows. Betty
produced the shows. She was really great. She produced all
these shows in the West End and all: underneath the arches
and all this sort of stuff. Of course, I used to play her up
something rotten. It was terrible, and she was trying to be
serious! I had them all in fits, you know what I'm like.
Every year there was a show put on and I did most of the
things on the show for them. The money went to the
Church. If you look at the programmes it's: Kevin
O'Connor this, Kevin O'Connor that, all the way along.
And I did some music with the guitar as well and they all
joined me, all the others from the show, and it was lovely,
you know? Every Tuesday, we used to go for rehearsal,
which was really fun. And Kathleen provided the food - the
sandwiches and all that type of thing.

It sounds like you did a lot of singing when you lived in

Shipston.
Yes, loads. But it started before that.

When did you first learn to play the guitar?
A long time ago, a very long time ago.

When you were a child?
Oh no - we couldn't afford things like that, pfffff! What?
No way. When I was older Jackie was into all that and I got
interested. Eventually I got this guitar - only a cheap bloody
thing but I loved it. He didn't teach me or anything; I was
self-taught, really. I picked it up myself, a bit at a time.
What I do is very rudimentary; I just do the three-chord
trick. It's only three chords: C, G and F but you can use it
for anything. I've had loads of guitars since then.

When did you start singing for money?
I don't remember exactly. It was mostly pubs in a few
places. Not fantastic places, just ordinary pubs. I didn't
have the mic or amp, nothing like that. I was in my
twenties, still, in Cheltenham, before Jane and the kids. I
used to sing but I'd need someone to play guitar or
keyboard. I played with Sharp - the one who attacked me
years later.

The one you nearly killed?
That's him. I played with him a few times. He was very
good on the guitar. Couldn't sing for toffee but great on the
guitar. We did alright, you know? I don't know what
happened. I think I moved away or something or we had
some disagreement or other.

When did you sing in public again?
It was at the Irving hotel, just before I met Kathleen. I
worked at the bar for a while, and while I was there, just for
entertainment, I used to sing for the people in the bar. Not
with me guitar or nothing, just singing while I was working.

196

Some of them said, 'Why don't you have a go and do a little sing for the people, you know?' Hmmmmm, alright then. So, one night I wasn't working behind the bar and I got in and I brought me guitar - no mic, just the guitar. I was singing away and there were a few people in, and I thought, I'm enjoying this, this is nice, you know? Anyway, there was these two or three chaps at the table, watching but I didn't think anything of it. When I'd finished my spot, or whatever you call it, they come to me and they said, 'We've been talking amongst ourselves and we are very impressed by what you did.' This was in the sixties, by the way. I thought, that's nice, thank you. They said, 'Well, we've formed a rock brand and we've just recently lost our singer and we'd be very interested in you joining us.' It was a real opportunity for me. But I, at that time was having trouble with Jane, my wife, with the kids and I had to decide - do that and put my whole mind into it which I would had do or fight for the kids. I decided to do the latter. And they went to the top, that rock group.

What were they called?
I can't remember.

Oh. I thought you were going to say The Beatles or something.
That would have been something!

It would. It would have made it a better story, certainly!
Ha! But the thing is, I missed a chance there, a golden opportunity. Not the Beatles maybe but they made it big, you know? The children were too important to me, you see?

I noticed you have a CD with you and someone else on the cover. How did that come about?
That was when we were in Cheltenham, Kathleen and me, before Shipston. I did a bit of singing on my own for a while until I thought, well, I'm fed up doing this thing on

my own, I want a bit of company. So, then I formed Emerald, my duo, with this chap. Phil he was called.

How did you meet him?
I advertised in the paper and he answered the ad. He was an absolute brilliant guitar player. Of course, that's what I wanted. I can sing, and I don't have to worry about the guitar. Phil worked in BMW, he had a really top job there - you know, the motor company? That's when they started to call me Kevin instead of Ronald. It was my idea. I thought, well, Ronald doesn't sound very Irish, you know? So, I started using it, calling myself Kevin and then everyone started calling me Kevin. I put it on my CDs as well. Kevin O'Connor was more Irish. There used to be a good singer years ago called Cavan O'Connor, and they said that's nice, about the name, you know?

Why did you call your duo 'Emerald'?
Phil, he said to me, 'What do you think we could call it?' And I said, 'Well, I think we could call it, as it is to do with Ireland,' - it's mostly Irish songs we did - I thought, 'why don't we call it Emerald?' And he said, 'That's a good idea.' We sang some lovely songs - Irish folk songs. A nice one, one of my favourites, 'Come Back Paddy Reilly' it's called.

> The garden of Eden has vanished they say
> But I know the lie of it still
> Just turn to the left at the bridge of Finea
> And stop it halfway to Coote Hill
> 'Tis there I will find it I know sure enough
> When fortune has come to my call
> The grass it is green
> Around Ballyjamesduff
> And the blue sky is over it all
> And tones that are tender and tones that are gruff
> Come whispering over the sea
> Come back Paddy Reilly to Ballyjamesduff

198

Come home Paddy Reilly to me

And you recorded some CDs?
Yes. The first was with Phil. 'A Touch of Emerald' we
called it. We decided to do something to look back on, you
know? It cost us a bit of money, but it was well worth it.
We hired the time in this studio for a few hours and, bless
her, the girl there, the woman there was just unbelievable.
She only had a keyboard but phoa, what she couldn't do
with that? She made that keyboard talk, she did.

She didn't make it sing?
Ha, ha. No, I was the one doing all the singing! But she as
amazing. If you listen on there you hear the backings that
she did for all the songs. There's a song on there, one of the
best ones, it's called 'The Old House' - you want to get a
chance to hear it. Fantastic backing, and it's an absolutely
beautiful song. Sad but lovely. It's saying about, years ago,
how the house used to have children in it; they're all gone
now. And the elderly people have long gone and there's no
welcome in the house anymore.

Oh, lonely I wander through scenes of my childhood
They call back to memory those happy days of yore
Gone are the old folk, the house stands deserted
No light in the window, no welcome at the door

Here's where the children played games on the heather
Here's where they sailed their boats on the burn
Where are they now? Some dead, some have wandered
No more to their home will the children return

Oh, lonely the house now, and lonely the moorland
The children have scattered, the old folk are gone
Why stand I here, like a ghost or a shadow?
'Tis time I was movin', 'tis time I passed on.

I actually had it played on the radio.

Which radio station?
Severn sounds. I went to their studio. They were based in
Cheltenham. They had a little a little, not an office - they
used to work the programme from there - in the actual
arcade, where the shops all are. I went in and told them
about this CD, and he said they'd have a whirl, have a go,
and he liked what he heard. So, they put me on air and gave
me an interview and all. And they played a few tracks off it,
including the one I said, 'The Old House'.

Did you sell the CDs?
Not those, no. The ones I sold were the ones which you've
done loads of copies of, which is great.

'Kevin O'Connor - Country and Folk'?
That's the one. I did that those on my own, it didn't involve
Phil. That was professionally done, in Shipston-on-Stour. I
saw advertised in the paper, Jennifer Trust and I thought I
want to do something. They help children that have got the
thing with the chest, you know? Spina bifida. They live to
be about eight or nine. They were looking for another
wheelchair, it said in the paper, and thought, I felt very
sorry for them, what can I do? Well, I was a lot better off
then so I thought, I know what I'll do. So, I went into the
studio and made that CD. You can see the Jennifer Trust
thing on there, on the CD case. And then I sold them all
round Shipston, you know, a fiver each. I made a nice bit of
money for the trust. A lot of the people there have still got
them, I imagine. All the friends we had there.

Where did you play live?
Everywhere, really. A very popular place was down the
Forest of Dean. They loved the Irish music down there.
Love it. We got quite a few gigs there. When the race week
was on, because the Irish come over, don't they? And we

had an agreement with the landlord there - he liked the rebel songs. You know, the ones you're not supposed to sing, but he wasn't bothered. Scottish but he loved the Irish rebel songs about the IRA and all that type of thing. The agreement was we were to go there, the same pub, the Swan, for four days over the race week and after that we got five hundred pounds each. We did really well. We videoed a lot of the shows we did. I'm going to get them put on the CD because there's a chap in the village up here, and he transfers to CDs for the DVD player.

Do you remember any of the rebel songs?
You're not supposed to sing them - they're about the IRA. The funny thing is, we were in the middle of this real rebel song, in the pub - who walks in? Six British soldiers! They were outnumbered, they couldn't do nothing because there were so many people there enjoying it. If they got too funny with the locals, they'd tear them to bits. So, we just carried on. There was so many songs we sang. One them was 'I'm off to join the IRA'.

I'm off to Dublin in the green, in the green
Where the helmets glisten in the sun
Where the bayonets clash and the rifles crack
To the sound of a Thompson gun

I'll leave aside my pick and spade and I'll leave aside my plough
I leave behind my old grey mare, for no more I'll need her now
And I'll take my short revolver and my bandoleer of lead
I'll do or die I can try to avenge my country's dead

I know I leave behind my Mary - she's the girl I do adore
And I wonder will she think of me when she hears the

canon roar?
And when the war is over and old Ireland, she is free
I'll take her to the church to wed and a rebel's wife
she'll be

And we're off to Dublin in the green, in the green
Where the helmet's glisten in the sun
Where the bayonets clash and the rifle's crack
To the echo of a Thompson gun

The Thompson gun, that's the English one, you know.

Why did you and Phil stop playing together?
I think he had some problem with his eyes. To do with the
sugar diabetes, or something.

Who did you perform with after that?
Alan Braybourne was his name. We got on really well. We
did this amazing gig one night - Felix Terbis was our guest:
he was brilliant on the fiddle. I've got it on tape, but I'd like
to get that put on CD. There's a video and Bernadette is on
there. She was there in the pub when the camera went
around. Would be nice to see her there. She came to a few
of them because she obviously enjoyed the music and
things.

Why did you and Alan split up?
What mucked that up was his wife. You know I'm allergic
to dogs?

You've mentioned it a few times, yes.
I went to the house and the dog decided to jump all over
me. Well, I wasn't having it and she got all stroppy about it
because I was reacting towards the dog. I said I have to go
outside, and she took it personally. But she was glad
enough for the money he was bringing in! 'Cos we were
doing really well. His missus, she got a bit funny. I suppose

she nagged him about me.

Did she not like you?
I don't know what it was. She was a bit funny, that's all. But there you go.

What other memories do you have from living in Shipston?
There was a worrying time with Kathleen's son, Lee. She nearly lost him. He'd got gangrene and they had to remove his toes. He was critical. They didn't think he'd make it. It was from smoking and drinking - mostly from smoking. He was rushed to hospital and he had tubes through here, tubes through there, and an oxygen thing because he couldn't breathe himself. He was in a mess, a right state, the poor lad. I went along with Kathleen, each time, to see him but his dad couldn't give two monkeys, of course. Anyway, I went over to him, he was like, not in a coma but he wasn't looking or anything like that. So, I put my hand on his hand there, on his arm, and I got a reaction. I mean a very, very strong reaction and I thought, hmmm. I said to Kathleen, 'This looks good. We'll see. I'm not saying anything, but this could be good.' My hands started to feel it and he started to move a bit, so he was getting a reaction too. I said, 'Don't worry Lee, you'll be alright, there you are love.' I went up a few times. There was a Chinese doctor there - she was brilliant - and she said it was amazing. He was at death's door and three days later he was up, with his dressing gown on and he walked up to us and gave us a hug. The doctors couldn't believe it, which is understandable. He recovered completely and it happened so sudden. I've no doubt at all, if I hadn't intervened, Lee would not be with us. Kathleen knew what was going on. She should know the effect too: her being used to being with me, she's getting this off me all the time.

Any other positive memories from around that time?
Definitely - we had a blessing for our marriage when we

203

were in Shipston. You're saying you're happy being married. When we got married, it was done in a registry office, so we wanted a blessing in Church. And we had two priests, not one, doing the service. These relations of Kathleen's, they let us use their house and our friends went to town. They put flowers all over the place. It was absolutely beautiful! A big meal was put on. They went all out they did. And they did it all for free. It was done on a shoestring, but it was lovely. Liam was alive then and he was there. And Sean was there and Bernadette and her boys. I've got it all on DVD, but I can't see it at the moment because it shows Liam there and it's a bit upsetting.

What made you leave Shipston?
We never should have left, really. We had a good life there, you know? We were very popular with all the people there. They were very kind, and we got to know them all. But we were still trying to use up our money from when we sold the house. One of the things we did is we got a lovely bath put in - shower and everything. But, but, the company that did it were a load of crooks. They fiddled us, basically. After a few months, we noticed that the bath was getting all horrible because it hadn't been glazed. Underneath where the bath was it was terrible. It was in a state: all rotten. So, we said to Orbit, they're the ones who do all the housing for the council, can you sort it, but they said, 'Oh, no, you bought the bath, you've got to replace it!' I thought we can't carry on living like this. That is one of the main reasons we left. What we should have done, in retrospect, we should have taken the bath out and paid for it all ourselves and have it done rather than what we did. It would have cost a few grand but we had the money and it would have been worth it. Instead, we left all our friends because we went up the North.

Where did you go?

It was a fatal mistake. We ended up in this prefab place in the middle of nowhere. Out in the wilds. Kathleen's son was up there. Her oldest son, Nick. He'd got a house up there and Kathleen said, 'I'd love to be by him.' It wasn't a proper house - it was a pre-fabs, which means they were only intended for people to live in during the war. They weren't meant for permanent living. The nearest shop was about half an hour. Lucky we had a car. Of course, we got caught in the winter, didn't we? And the only way you could heat the place was you had to get onto this lot, and they provided all the oil. Outside was this huge big, what do they call it? A boiler or whatever you like. You put all the oil in there, and it heats the bungalow and the water. There's no other way of doing it, no electric. There was electric but not in the respect of heating and so on. Only for your lights. They were the only company around so, of course, they charge as much as they want. It was supposed to keep us going through the winter and it cost us a grand. But it didn't last the winter. The woman who lived there before was very nice: she didn't leave any for us. She drained every last drop out! The other people around there, they were in clover because they had the heat from wood - big logs. The rich ones. The posh ones with the big four by fours. Not us, the riffraff, according to them. They looked down their nose at us.

What was it like, living there?
We tried to make it nice, you know? Kathleen's other son Lee, who was into decorating and all, he came along and he decorated the place for us. I helped him as well. Made it look nice. We got new carpets and all sorts of things to make the place habitable, you know? But, after a month or so, it was all riddled with damp. It was a bad winter. You'd look out and the snow would come up like that against the door outside, piled up high. The field was covered in snow as far as the eye could see. It was terrible, really. It was a nightmare. The carpets were all ruined. The damp was

crawling up the walls. For some reason, don't ask me why, it had millions of hairs in it! It didn't help Kathleen with her chest problems that she'd got, either. She's asthmatic and she developed COPD as well. It's to do with the lungs, you know? So that was the worst place to be in. Anyway, I got on to this health department and he was very helpful. He said, 'You can't carry on living like this up here, you know?' It wasn't fit for anything. So eventually, he got on to somebody else and we moved out. We'd had enough.

Where did you go next?
We came back then to Cheltenham for a while. We had a place there, a flat in Cheltenham itself, not on the outskirts. After that, we moved to Bidford.

Chapter 26

Bidford-on-Avon

When did you move from to Bidford?
That was three or four year ago. Two thousand and
seventeen it was.

Why did you decide to move there?
We just liked the flat, you know? Nice village and all that.

Was it because Donna lived there?
Not really, I don't think. But it was probably one of the
reasons. Donna was paying through the nose and the
landlord wouldn't do anything for her, but when she went
out the back, she had a nice view of the river.

How did you get on with the other people in the flats?
We got on really well, at first, with all the people there.
They bought us, because we were new, these lovely towels
for Christmas. They welcomed us so much. We got on and
all, and I sang in front of them and all. But one wasn't nice.
She was trouble. She's that type of person. Horrible
woman; a real bitch. None of the others would have
anything to do with her. Unfortunately, things went wrong
there after we'd been there a while.

More trouble with the neighbours? What was the issue?
I don't know what it was. Things just didn't go right. It was
the bitch woman. She caused a lot of trouble. Each person's
got their own spot for your washing, right? It's written on
the thing. You can be down there for an hour: that's your
slot. So, in that hour, I'd come down, put on the machine
and get washing in and then the other one would dry it. But
she started making problems, this woman, saying we were
going in her spot, which we weren't, and she got nasty with
Kathleen and had her in tears. Something about putting the
light off or some bloody crazy thing like that. She's a nasty
bit of work. And then she started stirring with the others.
Kathleen should have gone down to the knitting thing they
wanted her to do, but she didn't fancy going. That was her
choice, but she should have gone because it made matters
worse. That's how it started, really. After that, there was an
atmosphere. The trouble was, this woman had got this idea
in her head that she's in charge, right, because she goes to
some of the council meetings and it's gone to her head.

Did you challenge her about this?
Well, I did, eventually, yeah. I wouldn't put up with it. I
said to her, get a life, you know? But I couldn't change her.
She had this idea that she was above all the rest of us, but
she wasn't. She started stirring them all up and that was it,
really. She's a stirrer, a nasty bit of work. She ran us down
behind out backs and said things that weren't true. I don't
know what she was saying but it wasn't very pleasant living
there and then it started to get out of hand.

Did you meet people from outside the flats?
Yes, but it turned out to be a fatal mistake. We saw this ad
in one of the free papers. You know, the local paper which
has all the ads in it. It said, do you want your, what you call
it - all your stuff sorted, you know - decluttered. Well, after
thirty years you can imagine what we'd accumulated.
Everywhere there was bags of stuff. Not rubbish - some of

it was really good stuff - we just didn't have the room. It was only a one bedroom flat. It said phone this number. Biggest mistake we ever made. That's when Janet arrived on the scene. Her husband - her boyfriend because they were never married - he is a director of some company. They own some houses, but they rent them out to people. For some reason or other, her mum didn't want to have anything to do with her - that's neither here nor there, it's none of my business - but I think that's why she got on with Kathleen. Kathleen was like a mother figure to her.

Janet provided the de-cluttering service?
That's right, yeah. She got on to us and I gave her the two-hundred-pound that she wanted. And with that, she gradually started to get rid of some of the stuff, a bit at a time. She didn't dump it all because some of it was really good. She gave a lot of it to charity and all. And then we became really friends with her and her boyfriend. He's a really nice man. He's high up in some company, you know? Richard Bankcroft, he's called. They got rid of all the stuff and then they brought us things we needed for the flat. First, they came with that coffee table and I thought, that's really nice of them, you know? Anyway, they brought more things, bit at a time.

What else did they get for you?
Well, Richard, he was impressed by my singing. He loved me singing. He bought me a tablet and he helped with it to download some songs on there. Backing tracks and all, off of what's it called? Not Facebook, the other one: Spotify. I thought that was really nice of him. Over a hundred pound I 'spose. We were getting on great. Janet and Richard had become like part of the family. And then they got us some wardrobes. They tried to put the two wardrobes together. Absolutely beautiful they were - all glass doors with curtains behind them and all. They must have got them from somebody rich who died I suppose. But we couldn't

get the two wardrobes to fit properly so she said, 'I know who will help.'

Who was it?
Well, in Bidford, they have a thing. The neighbours all help each other, using the internet. If somebody wants somebody to walk the dog, they do that, if somebody wants someone to look after the children, they do that and so on. It's the way it is in Bidford, they will help each other, are you with me?

Yes, I'm a member of the group.
Oh yeah, of course, that's how we met you! Anyway, Janet knew straight away who to get on to when we couldn't get the wardrobe properly fitted. So, she got on her mobile and she phoned Paul, who is to do with the church. Within twenty minutes, he came along with his wife, Sarah. They came and they introduced us to them, and he sorted it out 'cos he's very clever, Paul is, with his screwdriver and all. I couldn't believe how lovely they are. You know, they cuddled us and all and I thought, what lovely people. Really nice, you know? That's how I got introduced to this religion thing, you know?

So, everything was going well?
We was all getting on well; everything was fine. We was having meals together and it was all lovely. So, I don't know what happened, but everything changed after that.

What changed?
It was Kathleen. She'd been OK for a while, her health I mean, but then we had a problem with the shower. You flushed the loo and it was coming up into the shower. It took them two months to sort that out. Two months! It was unhygienic, you know? I reckon Kathleen got a urinary infection because she started to change.

In what way?

She became very aggressive with me. She stayed up 'til one, two in the morning watching late night films instead of coming to bed and then sleeping in her chair. I didn't know what to do. All of a sudden, she started accusing me of things. That glass dish there - she said I'd broken that, because I do the washing up. I said, 'I haven't broken it.' 'Yes you have!' she said. 'If you haven't broken it, where is it then?' she said. I said, 'I don't know where it is.' It turned out Janet had borrowed it and hadn't told us. She came back with it in two days' time. Kathleen got in a state and said, 'You've made me like this!' She started crying - she was in a hell of a state. I didn't know what to do. This went on for weeks.

Did she see a doctor?

No, she said she didn't need to. She said I was the problem. Paul came along and we talked about me and Kathleen. About what I'd done and about what Kathleen had done. And things we said to each other - things we regretted. I had a word with the doctor, and they said, 'That sounds like she's got a urinary infection - from the shower.' They finally got that sorted but only after my MP had got onto them and written to them, and written to them, and written to them. By then the damage was done.

What do you mean?

Everything went wrong after that. I think Janet had a lot to do with it. Janet took to Kathleen. In a big way, I mean. Not in a sexual way. Shall we say - like a mother figure? She started saying things to Kathleen. They'd go out together to these posh coffee shops and what she was saying to Kathleen… I don't know but she was obviously saying things to her. Gradually, Kathleen started to get really, really funny with me. I couldn't do anything right. Then it came to a crunch.

What happened?

One day, we were in the kitchen and I went in and she pushed me. She pushed me backward - just like that. She got quite aggressive with me and I made the fatal mistake, which I shouldn't have done, I pushed her back. Not violent or nothing. With that then, she got on the phone, wawawawawa, to Janet, who obviously she's got on fast dial because she got through like that. They must have planned it between them, I reckon. Next thing is, the police arrive. This copper comes to the door. I was practising in the other room - my music, you know, getting the backings right, the timing and all. He said, 'Could I see you a bit, mister?' I said, 'Of course you can.' He said, 'Your wife's got on to us, but she's admitted she assaulted you first and therefore we wouldn't take it any further. But I would like you,' he said, 'to go into the spare flat, to stay there overnight until you've got things sorted.' Obviously, then, she was going to go with Janet. Next day, I came in and she said, 'What we have is gone now,' she said to me. I said, 'I don't think it has - it hasn't with me, anyway.' But there was nothing I could do. She'd made up her mind.

Why do you think she decided to leave?

She'd obviously been running me down with Janet, saying I'm no good and saying this, that and the other. Janet had done a good case of brainwashing her, I think, over a period of weeks. It was the infection that started it - that's what I reckon.

So, Kathleen moved out?

I haven't seen her since. Not once. I haven't even talked to her. I've tried to contact her but no luck, I'm afraid. Kathleen has an aunt who lives in Bidford, not far from where the pharmacy is, so I thought I'd write a letter and have it sent there, you know? And of course, Janet got funny with this and said, 'If you keep on doing this, we're going to take you to court.' She's the one that started the nasty things, shall we say? There was no need for that at all, you know? She turned it all nasty, Janet did. I wanted to still be friends with Kathleen after all that time.

Chapter 27

After Kathleen

How has the break-up affected you?
It's broken me, I tell you. It really has. It has affected me
really badly. I've got really down, you know, really
depressed. Came very near to ending it, I did. Very near.
Taking tablets. We'd been together so long and all. I miss
her so much, you know? I still do.

What stopped you from doing it?
I think the main thing is because of my religion. It's a
mortal sin, you know - taking your own life.

Has your faith helped you through it?
I think it has, yes, but not the church I went to before. I was
going to the Catholic church in Bidford, but I wasn't very
impressed. When Kathleen and I had split up, I talked to
father, you know, the priest, and he didn't really want to
know. He wasn't interested, I could tell. And I got the
impression he was siding with Kathleen more than me. You
see, he'd heard all these stories - they were all round
Bidford - all a pack of lies.

Did you try any other church?
Well, Paul had mentioned this church he went to, for born-

again Christians. The Barn, it's called. It was just around the corner, really. Five minutes around the corner. At first, I wasn't really interested but we got to know Paul and Sarah and they brought one of these children up - their son or a friend or something, one of Sarah's relations, I think - who was into their religion. They all sat there, and I sang these songs, these religious songs I was doing, and they all loved it. And it went from there.

Did you go to The Barn regularly?
I went there most weeks, but not all. The people were lovely, very friendly, but it was so noisy. Lots of singing and clapping and it was too much for me. But I got used to it and it became a comfort, you know? They helped a lot and were very good - they helped me out with things. They were very understanding where I didn't get that from my own church, the Catholic church.

Have you tried to contact Kathleen since the break-up?
Paul knows where she lives but he won't tell me. I don't blame him, really. He's protecting Kathleen and I respect that. He acted as a go between for a few months, between Janet and Kathleen and me. He was bringing back messages and things. But then Kathleen started saying things to him. I don't know what she said but I think she was making things up. Making up stories that I was supposed to have beat her up which is not true again. She had bruising on her legs but that was caused by the tablets that she took when she had that heart attack. The tablets that she had can cause bruising and she was trying to blame me for that, saying I'd kicked her and all. I told Paul this and eventually he said, 'I'm not going to act as go between anymore. I can't stand people telling lies.'
Has Kathleen tried to contact you?
Not me, no. But she wrote to my sister, Patricia, in Canada, running me down. A four-page letter she wrote. Patricia wouldn't put up with it. She knows it's not true. My sister

wrote back to her and sent the letter to Janet, because she didn't know where Kathleen is living. Kathleen was living with Janet for a while then she went into bed and breakfast, I believe, and then the council gave her a place, but I don't know where.

How long did you stay in the flat after Kathleen left?
I didn't want to stay. There we too many memories of Kathleen. And I didn't feel comfortable there anymore. Janet was saying things about me. It was all around to the shops and everything, all around Bidford. Janet, her being very well off like she is and all, they listen to her, don't they? A few of them were acting funny with me and all. The others were alright because they thought: I don't believe what I've heard. A few of them there were really off with me. I complained about one of the girls, in Budgens, because she was so off with me and the manager, who I got on great with, he said if she didn't stop, he'd do something. She never said anything, but she didn't have to, you know what I mean?

What did she do?
Well, she was looking at me funny and acting funny when she was dealing with me and all. And I got fed up with it in the end. And this tall chap, tall bloke, about six two, six three, he was really off with me because he's been told things. He didn't say anything, but I could tell, he was looking at me like something you'd lost on your shoe, you know? Everyone had heard these things about me.

Are you sure you weren't being a bit paranoid?
No because it was happening all the time. I had this chance with this really lovely girl, woman. She owned this caravan park, so she must have been loaded, but I wasn't interested in that. She was dead interested in me but then she made some enquiries and she heard about me and that was it. Wouldn't answer me anymore, so that was ruined. And I

used to see people in the streets looking like this: that's him! That's him! It's not very nice, especially when you're not guilty and you can't answer, you know? So, my name was mud there. Not with everybody, obviously but a lot of the people so I had to go.

So, where did you go next?
I looked for somewhere else and I moved to this bungalow in Wellesbourne. The place I'm in now.

Do you still go to The Barn?
No, I've started to go to the church at Redhill because it's nearer, but it's run by the same people as The Barn in Bidford. That's where I met Phil, and we've been great friends ever since. I've been quite worried about him, but he called to say he's in the clear. He's been ill, you see? I'm hoping, but I don't really know, that I've had something to do with it. Every time I see Phil - he's such a warm person - I always cuddled him. Maybe that did something, but I don't honestly know. I'm not going to be presumptuous and say I might of helped him.

Have you kept up with Kathleen's children?
Not with her son, no. Her eldest son, Nick, he never wanted me to be with her in the first place. He never approved of me. Nick's a bully but he couldn't bully me because I did the martial arts. He tried, but I wouldn't put up with it, you see, and he didn't like it. It got a bit chopsy, put it that way, but he never tried to do anything because he knew I wouldn't tolerate it. The sons all said I was a karate freak. They didn't like it because they had to respect me whether they liked it or not, because they couldn't mess with me. Obviously, I can see their point. I'd broken their marriage up, with their dad. I don't blame them really.

What about Donna?
I've known Donna since me and Kathleen got together. She

was eleven. And she remembers what I was like with Kathleen because her dad was never like that. He treated Kathleen terrible, but I loved her, and Donna knows that. So, I got to know her, and I still talk to he sometimes. I don't think she agrees with her mum and me splitting up. I saw her about a months after me and Kathleen left. I was doing a gig, for charity, at The Frog pub in Bidford and she came up to me and gave me a big hug and a cuddle and all, so she made it clear she doesn't hold anything against me. She's had a hard life, of course, Donna has.

In what way?
She got in with this one called Wookie, who is a drug pusher.

Wookie? Isn't that from Star Wars?
Don't ask me where he got that name from. He was a low life, anyway. She had two children from him. Two girls. He was encouraging her to mess with drugs and was using her all the time and she couldn't get away from him, you know? She took to the drink and she got into all sorts of trouble. She was in the car one day, Donna was, with the girls, and she'd been drinking, and she went mad with driving properly, so the car turned over like that. Social services turned up and they took the kids, the girls. They were in care for a year or two but they're back now and they seem to have forgiven her. She managed to get away from Wookie in the end, but it caused a lot of friction and that's why Mark, that's Kathleen's younger son, wouldn't speak to her. Apparently, she borrowed some money and didn't pay it or something.

Where does Donna live now?
She lives in Bidford. She's got a house there with her boyfriend. She delivers things for one of the delivery companies, parcels and so on. Her boyfriend sells antiques and all and she gave him a boy which he wanted to carry on

218

his business. I think that's where Kathleen's living: in Bidford, with Donna, helping with the baby. Either that or she's moved near her, that's what I reckon.

OK, I think we've done enough for today.
I think so too.

I think we should do this by phone next week, because of the virus. You know - social distancing.
Yeah, I know. Everyone needs to stay at home if they can. It was on the telly. It's got much worse hasn't it?

It has. Italy, France and Germany are already in lock down. I think we'll be next.
I haven't been able to get any soap. I buy Wright's Coal Tar Soap and I can't find it in Sainsbury's or the Co-op.

Coal tar soap? That sounds like something from the second world war!
I never use anything else. I use it in the shower. You can't beat it.

Well, you'll be lucky to find any kind of soap at the moment.
Is it really that bad?

It is. No soap, no pasta, flour or eggs, no tinned vegetables. And worst of all, no toilet rolls!
I've got a spare one if you need it.

No! Keep it. You might need it, especially if you can't go out the shops.
I can still get to the shops alright!

Yes, but you shouldn't. You might catch the virus.
OK, I won't go shopping then.

Tell me if you need anything and I'll get it and drop it off

on your doorstep.
You won't come in at all?

Best not to.
You better step back then!

And definitely no hugging.
That's sad.

Alright, I'm off.
OK. Now you don't do anything silly. You look after yourself, alright?

Will do. Bye Kevin.
Bye.

Chapter 28

Today

Hello?
Hello, is that Dan?

Yes, it is.
I'm glad you've called. 've not spoken to anyone in a while.

I'm sorry to hear that.
You're the only one that's been in contact since the lock down. Not even the ones at the church.

That's a pity.
They're supposed to be a community, you know?

I expect they have lots of things to worry about at the moment. This virus is affecting everyone.
I know. It's worrying isn't it?

Are you OK for food?
I've got enough for the time being but not much.

I'll find you the number of your local support group. They'll make sure you get a food delivery, or I can do it.
Oh, thanks. At least I have someone I can rely on.

Yes, you do.
You're my best friend, you know that?

Yes, I do. I'll make sure you're OK.
I know. So, are you OK with work at the moment?

Er, not really. It's all dried up, I'm afraid. Nobody wants face to face training at the moment!
That's not good.

Don't worry. I have my savings.
Well, I hope you're alright?

I am.
That's good.

And, at least this book is keeping me busy.
How's it coming along? It's not easy remembering so much. I think I've not done too bad, have I, considering? I've tried my best, anyway.

You've been brilliant. You've remembered sixty thousand words!
I can't believe that, honestly! Or what-d'you-call-him says 'I dooon't believe it'.

Victor Meldrew?
That's the one. Oh, I love that man - talk about funny!

I doooon't believe it either!
How will we get it published?

I'm not sure yet. We could self-publish on Amazon I suppose.
That would be good.

222

We'll see. Let's see if we can finish it today, shall we?
Why not?

I think we've talked about your whole life up to the present day.
It was quite hard to remember everything, but we got there in the end, didn't we?

You have a great memory! But today, could we talk about what your life is like now?
What do you mean?

How do you spend your time?
Well, I've done well to get this bungalow. All the problems in Bidford - with the shower and with Kathleen and I splitting up and everything - I think Orbit knew a lot of it was their fault. I think that's why they decided to give me this bungalow, which I was really surprised to get. A two-bedroom bungalow - they're about as rare as hen's teeth! I think they had a bit of a conscience, shall we say, and decided to try and make it up to me as best they could. But I also think, and you might think this is ridiculous, I also think it has lot to do with Jesus as well. I think he was at that meeting when they decided to give me this bungalow and believe it or not, he persuaded them. It's up to you what you believe but I think that's what happened. He put a word in good word shall we say? It's unheard of to give a two-bedroom bungalow to somebody on their own, but they did. And it's only four mile from Stratford.

Who helped you move in?
The ones from the church, The Barn. They came here and they saw what it was like. Phil was very good - he put things up like the curtain rails and he also mowed, even though you can't tell now, he mowed the garden, which was lovely then, after he'd done it. And Mary, that's Phil's wife, she's the one that gave me these table and chairs, you

know? They've been really marvellous. The Royal British legion gave me the carpets.

Because you served in the army?
Yes. I wasn't in the army for long but they're good like that. I couldn't afford any carpets you see? It cost me over three hundred pound to move and I was very, very hard up then and Mary went and said to Phil, 'Here, give him that,' and she gave me two hundred pound. She borrowed me two hundred pound and that got me out of a real tight spot. I owe her twenty-five, I think, but I've paid her back the rest now. I don't like owing people money.

How do you get on with your new neighbours?
Some of them around here are really nice. Him next door, he's alright. He's on his own. He's got no kids or nothing. He gave me, which he didn't have to do, he gave me the line you know, over there, the proper thing? It opens up for your washing when you put your washing on, you see it there? It's got a cover on at the moment.

The whirligig?
Well, I don't know what they are but they're very expensive anyway, but he gave me it for nothing. He likes his cake so every so often he comes in and he stays for an hour or two for a natter and things.

Have you met any other neighbours?
Well you've got the other couple and he's only started speaking to me recently. He's alright but the wife's a right misery. She wouldn't talk or nothing; she was really off. They just keep themselves to themselves, I suppose, just not very friendly, you know? Further up, there's another couple and they'd not really friendly either. It's a type of snobbery: we've got a house, you haven't, you know? Little do they know that I had two houses at one time. We'd still have them now if we'd had no win no fee. We had witnesses and

224

everything and we'd have taken that man for thirty, forty grand.

What do you do to pass the time when you're in the bungalow?
I sometimes listen to the backing tracks that you've done for me, getting the timing just right. And sometimes I get the guitar out. It depends what mood I'm in, you know? I got to be in a reasonably good mood to feel like singing and I haven't been in that good a mood recently. I miss Kathleen terrible, you know. I mean she doesn't bother, I don't suppose, but I miss her.

Do you use your tablet much?
I use it all the time. Without that I don't know what I'd do because I'm on me own. I'm here at night on me own, there's nobody around, and it's company. It really is, you know? It's like a thing to the outside world, really. When I'm in here, that tells me what's going on. Something comes on there and it says breaking news, so you know what's going on. Some things on there are not very nice, but you've got to accept that. That's how the world is, I'm afraid. There was a thing on there a few weeks ago that was disgusting. It showed these two blokes that need to be shot. They'd got these dogs and they'd strung them up by the rope - hanging them like that. They catch them on there, and you press if you want it to go viral, you know, to show them up, which is what we need. They need to be shown up, the cruel things they do.And you get the odd girl, woman on there showing everything they've got but that's another story! They come on there and say, you know, we'd like to meet you and they keep going on about their pussy. But I've no interest in cats so I don't know why they keep banging on about their pussies! But they show them anyway, if you know what I mean? But that's part of life, init?

225

Which apps do you use most?
I'm on Facebook a lot. A hell of a lot, in fact. It's quite
entertaining, actually, a lot of it. There's quite a lot of
religious things on there. I mean there's a message there - I
don't even know where it's come from - but it said they've
heard I'm not happy or something and somebody's put my
photo on there and I don't even remember having that
taken. I have said to people there, on Facebook, that I'm not
happy but I'm not sure how they got back to me. I'm not
happy but I don't see that it's anyone else's fault. It's not
your fault, or anybody else's fault that Kathleen and I split
up. I take full responsibility. I say to Jesus all the time, I say
to him, and he knows how I feel. It's entirely, entirely my
fault. I'm not blaming Kathleen. I'm not blaming Janet. I'm
not blaming anybody - just me. I should have looked after
her better. I tried my best but obviously, it wasn't enough,
was it? You know, I gave her all the love I could, and I
always made sure she had things at Birthdays and
Christmases, but what else can you do? If I do get
somebody else, which I probably will eventually, I'll try to
do better, you know?

Are you seeing anyone at the moment?
There's this lady who's very interested in me at the
moment. She from Syrias. She lost her husband about two
year ago. It's a lovely lady.A lovely, decent lady, you
know? She wants to marry somebody. We're getting along
really good. She's in Liverpool at the moment. I don't
know how far that is. What do you think - you're better on
things like that?

*Let me check on Google. About two and a half hours by
car.*
But on train it'd be nothing. I could take a train and I've got
the bus pass. The distance obviously hasn't bothered her
because she'd looked at my profile so she knows where I
live so she must be keen. It says on there, how old I am,

that I'm divorced and everything. I don't smoke, I don't drink, things like that.

You need to be careful - people on the internet aren't always who they say.
I know, I know. I promise to be careful!

Have you taken up any new pastimes?
Well, I tried going with this walking group. I was nearly crippled after it. I had these boots. Lovely boots, they were but I've given them to a charity now. The trouble is they were brand new. I nearly crippled my feet! I haven't been since. And I went to this exercise class. This woman put in the paper, 'use it or lose it' was what she said. That was in Tiddington, up the road from here, not far - near Stratford. Will I ever forget?

Did something happen?
Well, she was really nice on the phone. I told her about Kathleen and everything. She used to be a psychologist, so she knew all about things, what makes people tick and that. I told her all about what happened when I lost my boys, you know, and she was really good on the phone, really understanding.

This was when you called her to ask about the course?
Yes. She said, 'You really have been through it.' I said, 'I know, but there's nothing I can do, that's the way it is, you know?' I told her all about my life and all: when I was younger, when I lost the children and everything. She was really understanding, and I thought, oh - she's going to be good! Anyway, I went there the first morning for the first thing and she was like a totally different person.

In what way?
She was just so cold. I was talking with the others and some of them were asking me questions. Some of them were

227

really nice, and I gave them a few of my cards - the ones you do for me - saying how I do country singing and all. Apparently, she didn't like that, because they were business cards, even though they were nothing to do with exercise. They're only to do with my music. It's a case of nit-picking, shall we say? Then we started doing the exercise and, of course, she played some of the songs I knew! Of course, what did I do? I started singing along with them, didn't I? Simon and Garfunkel - you know that one? What's it called, one of their nice ones.

Bridge over troubled water?
No, not that one - a different one. Then she played another one I know, 'Time goes by, so slowly' - that one. Anyway, we were doing these exercises, right, and I started singing away and she didn't like it. Some of them were loving it, really enjoying it but some of them there didn't like the singing and they made a complaint. She sent me a text saying don't come back to the thing and all. Quite rude. It was silly. Just because some of them complaining! I think she wanted all the attention, shall we say, and I took bit of attention off her and they all said, 'Woah, what a voice!' Oh yeah, they were impressed. Shame I couldn't go back, really.

Do you still go to The Barn each week?
Yes, I go every week. Of course, they've closed it now, because of the virus. But it has become very important to me.

Have you always been a religious person?
Well, I was brought up a Catholic, of course. I believed in god, obviously, but I wasn't sure if I believed it or not, if you know what I mean?

You mean you weren't sure God existed?
Not really. It was just a case of you went to church because

228

you were told to go to church, and I used to love singing. And school didn't sort of ram it down our throats, shall we say. Really, it was more just the lessons, the R.E. lessons. So, before I went to The Barn, I was about fifty, fifty I suppose. That's the best way to describe it.

When did you start to truly believe?
It was when I went over to this other religion, when I went to The Barn, just a few years ago now. I started to notice things happening, after I did this course.

What course?
Alpha course, it's called. Every week, so many of us would go to his house, Darren's house. A beautiful house, massive. He's in charge of it all, Darren is - The Barn and everything. He's a doctor. He's well off but he's not a snob. He's really down to earth and he's very much into his religion. And I sort of think, well, he's a doctor, if he believes these things then there's got to be something in it.

What did Alpha course involve?
It was really good. I'm really glad I did it. It woke me up, put it that way. It made me realise there is something. We can't see it but there's something there, definitely. And all these people were so into it and they were so kind. 'Cos I'd split up with Kathleen then and they were so understanding.

What happened in the classes?
He puts videos on, of different things, showing around the world, different people, religions and things and saying about God and everything.And we'd talk, of course, we'd discuss things. There was one chap there, he came there, and he didn't believe in anything. I mean, nothing. Whatever you said, he said the opposite. But even he was starting to, I think, believe there was something in it. I was having problems then, with the car, and he was very good,

and he picked me up and took me there in the evening and
he'd bring me back to the flat in Bidford. Lovely lad. He
was called Kevin, believe it or not!

Best not to trust him then.
Ha ha! You're not wrong. Never trust a Kevin, that's what I
always say.

How long did the course last?
It went on for months. I was a bit sad when it ended
because we always used to meet together, and she, his
missus - a lovely lady, a real sweetie, they're well matched,
her and Darren - she used to do a big meal for us. No
charge. The ones that run the thing, they pay her. Beautiful
meal. Not a little meal either, she went all out. I got on
great with them and because Kathleen and I had split up, I
was glad of the company, really.

How has the course affected you?
It has really helped. I've also noticed another thing that
never used to happen before, so I know he's listening. I've
explained to them in my church and they said, 'Well, that's
good!' I get sort of a feeling - how can I explain it to you?
It's like a sort of a, not a tingling, no. Do you ever get a
feeling, as people say, that sounds like somebody has
walked over my grave?

I'm planning to be cremated
Oh - you know what I mean!

Like a chill?
That's it. But it's nice. I get that a lot! I never used to ever
have that before. But then I never talked to Jesus before, did
I?

When do you get this feeling?
It depends. For example, he knows at the moment I'm

230

worried about Patricia, my sister. He knows that and when I had my breakfast this morning, I felt it. So, I know he ne must be listening. It's a really nice feeling, to know he's there. I know he's present. He's letting me know. In fact, it's just starting now, actually.

The feeling?
It's just coming up now. Ooh. Mmmm. Mmm. Right up my back now. Right up to my neck. Uh-huh. I don't know what that is now. Alright Jesus, I know. Oeff. All sort of cold feeling it was. I mentioned Patricia, you see?

What do you think it means?
It could either good or bad, you know?

What was the feeling like this time?
It's like cold, sort of, but it's not unpleasant. Like as shiver feeling, that's the best way to describe it. It only lasts a certain length of time. It's wearing off now, you see. It was just for a few seconds there. He lets me know that he's there, that he's present. I feel as if I've got somebody I can rely on and somebody that I know I love and he loves me, you know? It's very important. I never had that in my own church at all.

Chapter 29

Thinking back and looking ahead

Do you think you might fall in love again?
I hope so. I still love Kathleen, but I know she doesn't feel
the same. I have a lot of love to give so I hope I'll meet
someone. As it happens, I've got friendly with a lady in
Coventry recently.

What happened to the one in Liverpool?
She turned out to be another time waster I'm afraid.

How did you meet the woman in Coventry?
Just on the internet, the tablet - the app for meeting people.
She's really nice. She's got a terrific sense of humour
which I like, you know? I had her pissing herself laughing!

How embarrassing.
Not actually pissing herself, obviously! She's from - where
is it? Some country, I don't know, where they grow
bamboo. So, on there, she was down as The Bamboo Girl!
She lost her husband about four year ago and he was very
much into music, she said, so I sang her a few things and
she said, 'Oooh, you're good!' she said. Out there in
Coventry is where she lives - that's not that far, is it? That's
nice and near. 'I saw these buskers there,' she said, 'and I

thought they're not a touch on you,' she said. I thought that was nice.

Are you going to see her, do you think? After the virus has gone away?
I wouldn't want to go there now, anyway, the weather has been so cat.

Cat?
Yeah. It's been terrible, hasn't it? Never heard that expression?

No.
You're learning all these Irish expressions.

I've heard of 'raining cats and dogs' but not 'cat'.
Well, you can pay me later!

Thinking back over your life, what is the achievement you are most proud if?
The fact of having my children who I love all very much. I'm quite proud of them. They were all wanted, you know, they weren't accidents. And I'm proud of doing things for charities. I've done several gigs for the Shakespeare Hospice to make them money because they do terrific work. I did an open mic at The Frog recently and the one there said, 'You were really good,' she said and I said, 'Well, if you want me to do a gig, just let me know and all the money will go to the Shakespeare Hospice' because her mum's mum was helped by them. 'Just write a cheque for them,' I said.

Are you planning to raise more money for charity?
What I'm planning to do in the summer, if I can get that thing working eventually, you know? The backing things you did for me, instead of on the tablet, if I could get it onto the phone? If we would transfer them somehow - you know

how clever you are. I'm going to get on to either the cancer research people or the air ambulance. I want to get their own buckets. They have special buckets, right, that you can't tamper with or nothing. I've got to get a special licence, but I mean, there is no better place than Stratford for that. It's perfect, really. You get a lot of very rich people coming along there and people from all walks of life, you know? I'd soon get a nice bit of money for them.

You've raised lots of money for charity. Have you considered singing to make money for yourself?
I'm not that interested in money, really. Just so long as I know as I can get by, I'm quite happy. I've always said, because I do speak to Jesus by the way - I know you might think it's crazy but it's the way that I am - that if I won the Lottery, I'd give most of it away. I'd make sure you and Phil both had nice houses and I'd give a lot of it to charities for children who are sick.

What else are most proud if?
I think the fact I got to Strasbourg. That is my greatest achievement because I didn't give up. It took me five years to get there and I had to go through all the courts in England. Everybody said, including my solicitor, you'll never get there, nobody has ever has. Nobody had taken the United Kingdom government to Strasbourg. I'm the first one that did that.

What are least proud of?
I'm not proud of the fact that I didn't do enough with Kathleen to make her stay. I should have. I tried my best but obviously I didn't do enough for her. I took her for granted and I'm not proud of that. I shouldn't of, but it's too late now. I wrote to her and told her how I felt, and I also said I'd found Jesus. I told her I'm not the same person I used to be, which I don't think I am, and hoped that she'd forgive me, you know? And also, I don't hold any grudge

against Janet, even though she did break my marriage up.

I think that's really good!
At one time I did. I hated her. That's another thing I learned in that course: you don't want to hold grudges against anybody because, when you think of it really, it's just self-defeating, isn't it? It doesn't help, hating doesn't help. All that it is, it burns you up, you know? And I'm a great believer in karma, you know: what goes around, comes around, so it's not my job to deal with Janet. Somebody else will, one day, maybe.

Do you feel bitter at all about what life has thrown at you?
Pffffffff. I suppose a little bit, yeah.

What about?
Well, about losing my children. And Bernadette stopping me seeing the grandchildren. That affected me quite badly. Very badly. That was like a second chance for me. I idolised them. I got on great with them. But now they're nearly grown up and I haven't seen them for so long. I feel it when I see people with their grandchildren. I just have to bite my tongue and say, well... you know what I mean?

Yes, Kevin, I do.
It's just repetition, really, of what happened with my kids, in't it really? It's losing again. Being deprived of them, you know? It was a second chance, but it didn't last long. I sometimes wonder if I'm cursed, or something, for something I've done that's terrible bad in a former life or something. I don't know.

Have you tried to contact Bernadette or the boys?
Lots of times. I've tried contacting the boys with Facebook, but they won't talk to me, because she's poisoned them, unfortunately.I've missed out a lot with the boys, you know. It would be nice if Bernadette was to come back to

me and start having some relationship because obviously, I still love her and I miss her, you know?

Do you think she might come back?
She came back before after those twelve years so she might come back again. I'm just hoping and praying I make contact with her and boys again. I want them to know that I'm not seeing them not through my choice, which is true. I'd like to see them. I never would have liked for this to have happened. That's why I'm going to try and go over to Gloucester some time and just hope that I bump into Zak, you know? Morgan is a different kettle of fish - he's got a thing wrong with him. He's not mental or anything but, what's is called? Bergerism or something like that? Morgan's got that. They can't tell a lie. They don't know what it is to tell a lie. Everything's got to be exactly right. That's the way they are. It's not a mental thing, he's not mental or anything, but he's had to have special counselling and things for it. Morgan has got a little one, now. I know because a few months ago, it showed him on the internet, on Facebook I think it was, with this little one and it's just like looking at Morgan. I think it's a little girl, who I would love to get to cuddle if I could.

Do you have any other regrets?
Getting in with the wrong woman, definitely. Jane. They warned me but I didn't listen. My biggest regret is my children going into care. They all were affected by going into care. Anybody tells you they don't change - but they do. They're never the same after. I still say Ronald and Liam would be around now if they hadn't of gone into care. I don't think it, I know it. Because I'd have brought them up and they wouldn't have got involved in drugs because I'm not like that. They wouldn't have a bad example from me.

Any other regrets?
I regret Kathleen and I never had any children. Kathleen

couldn't, unfortunately - it wasn't her fault. She had the hysterectomy or something, which then, they were very keen on doing. This was before she met me. We'd have loved to have one, but it wasn't meant to be, I'm afraid.

Do you think you and Kathleen will ever get back together?
I know we will. I've seen Kathleen in that kitchen and I'm showing her around and she's saying, that's nice and all and then I cook her a meal and all. How it's going to happen or when it's going to happen, I don't know but it will happen. I know it will. That's what I've seen. Or is it wishful thinking? I don't think so because usually when I see things, they usually happen.

What do you miss about Kathleen?
Everything, really. Everything. There's never a day goes by I don't miss her. It's like a part of me is missing, you know? That's what it feels like to me. It's hard to describe. The company and also, I'm quite a loving person and I've got nobody to give my love to and my affection to. I always remembered her birthdays and Christmas. She always had jewellery, you know? Going back a few years now, I saw these pearls in this window in a shop called Martins - he's not there now. A very posh shop. I saw these pearls in there, and they were reduced from a thousand to five hundred. Real pearls I mean, not the artificial ones. They're like pink, a pinky colour. 'I can't afford them now,' I said, 'but would you allow me to put some money off, each week?' He said, 'Yeah, no problem,' so that's what I did. I put money off week after week, month after month and when Christmas came, I had just about enough paid off, so I paid the rest and I got her those.

Did she like them?
She was pleased with it, obviously, who wouldn't be? I always used to say, she's got more jewellery that Elizabeth Taylor! And the last lot of jewellery I got her, it was sent

back, of course. That's because of Janet. She sent it back saying Kathleen didn't want it. That was after we split up, of course.

Are there any songs that make you think of Kathleen?
Yes - there are a few songs that are particularly important to me, since Kathleen left. There's one that's higher than I normally sing but I tried it. It's one of Roy Orbison's ones: 'Too Soon to Know', it's called. When is says my hearts been broken in so many places, you know?

It's a beautiful song.
It is, isn't it?

Why does that mean a lot to you?
Well, it says the words about someone leaving someone, you know? After Kathleen and I split up, I heard this song and I loved it. I thought it was so lovely and it meant so much to me as well. The other one that means a lot to me is 'You're the only good thing that's happened to me'. That's Jim Reeves, of course. The other Jim Reeves one that's very important to me, I love it, it's really nice, it's called 'I know that I won't forget you'. He says, 'I've loved you too much for too long'.

Again, is that because it makes you think of Kathleen?
Of course it is, yeah. 'Cos I can feel it, in the singing, you know want I mean? It's my way of expressing myself, really.

Have you ever written any songs?
Just one. I wrote this song about Kathleen, after she left. There's this lady that phones me, you see, to do with depression and all. She works for Silverline. Lives up in Wales. They picked her out because we've got similar interests. Every Wednesday she phones from seven to half seven and we talk about music. She plays the guitar and

238

sings, and she's written a few songs and all and she said, 'Why don't you try to write a song?' I said, 'Nah, no chance, I've never done that before.' 'Well, why don't you have a go, you never know?' she said. Anyway, I was thinking about it and I was sitting here a few days after I'd talked to her and something came into my head. This song, about Kathleen. It goes like this:

I wrote this song, when you made me cry
I wrote this song, when you said goodbye
I wrote this song, 'cos I love you still
I wrote this song, because I always will

And now I'm alone and oh so sad
I think of the good times we had
I hope you hear this little tune
I wrote it specially for you

I wrote this song so the world will know
Just how much I love you so
I loved you then and I love you still
And I always have, and I always will

The strange thing was, when it came into my head and I started singing it, I sang it in a different voice, not my normal voice. Isn't that weird? How can you explain that?

I don't know. Maybe you want to make it special, for Kathleen?
Maybe.

What would you say to Kathleen now, if you could?
I love her and obviously I want to be by her and be with her. It's nothing to do with sex; it's pure affection, really. I love her and that's why I wrote the song. The girl from the church heard it - she came up here last weekend and I did them some chicken - and she said, 'That's very nice but it's

239

a bit sad.' I said, 'Well, I was sad when I wrote it, you know?' 'It makes me want to cry,' she said, and maybe that's good - it shows that it was affecting her, you know?

Having had so many life experiences, what is most important to you today?
I look for people that I know I can trust. That's very important. And also, people that have got good manners, that's very important, because I was brought up like that. You know my mum - I can still see her now - she always used to say it: civility costs nothing. And she was right. And I also remember her saying to me, when I was only seven or eight, she said, 'You know Ronnie, you could charm the leaves off the trees!' I can get around people. They all know me at the doctor's, you know? One lady there, I sing the Elvis one to her, 'The Wonder of You'. She loves that and you can see the people in the waiting room and they're going, ooh where's that coming from? It makes their day! I love that. And also, I tell them jokes and things. But I'm feeling, maybe, that I want to scream inside. I do, honestly, sometimes: I feel I want to scream. That's what I feel like, because I'm so down, but I won't let other people see that, are you with me? So, I put on this act. The doctor knows. 'You're a ruddy good actor,' she said. She's got me weighed up. 'I know exactly what you're like, Mr O'Connor, you don't fool me!'. 'I said, well, how else can I cope, you know?'

What else is important to you?
I like people that care about other people and not being selfish. I try to be a bit like that. I care. I hope so, anyway. I don't mind giving things to people; I don't expect things back. Those type of people I get on with, you know? I mean the lady up here in the local shop, she's an ambassador, she was telling me, to childhood cancer. I said, 'I tell you what I'll do then, I do a gig to raise money for you. I don't charge anything at all, if it's for charity.' Anything to do

240

with children, I do for free. I feel so sorry to see the little one with tubes coming out of them. Awwww, it really upsets me, very much. I'm a child lover, you know. I wanted all my children, but I got in with the wrong woman, that's the trouble, and lost them all because of her. That's my biggest regret. That and losing Kathleen of course.

What are your biggest hopes for the future?
Well, I want to get somewhere with my music, my country music. Make an impression, shall we say, because a lot of country singers are older than I am, you know? It's not like pop music where you've got to be a certain age. I'm only guessing but I think my voice is better now than it was ten year ago. That's only my opinion. It's a lot deeper, I know that much. I've heard my CDs and my voice is definitely a lot lower than it was then, and richer maybe?

That's good for country singing isn't it?
Exactly, yes, that's right, yeah.

You want your singing to take off somehow?
I'm hoping. I would like it to, yeah. Also, it's wishful thinking, I 'spose, but I'm hoping Kathleen and I will see each other again one day. Now, I know Kathleen will not come back, I know that. That's out of the question. But I'd like us to be friends again. And be something, maybe in her life. Whether it will happen, I don't know. That's the reason I wrote the song because that says a lot, on there.

Where do you see yourself in five years' time?
Well, I think I'll still be alive if that's what you're asking! I'm still fit and healthy, on the whole. Just so long as I don't catch Coronavirus, of course.

Well, Kevin, I think we've done it. We talked about your whole life!
Well, almost. Haven't you forgotten something?

What's that?
You! We haven't talked about you, really.

Oh yeah!
You're a big part of my life, of course you are, and have been for a long time now. Not just a matter of weeks or months.

It's been a couple of years.
Exactly, yeah.

OK, imagine I wasn't here and you're just describing your story as you have been doing. How did you meet me?
I was living in Bidford. And a very good friend of mine, who introduced me to their religion and all, Sarah, she told me about you because I was looking for somebody who was very clever, which you are, very clever at IT and all that type of thing. I needed somebody like that badly. 'I know a chap, he's really good,' she said, and that's how I started, you know? You've helped me with my tablet. I wouldn't have been able to do that - getting those songs, those backing track on there, which is really great, you know? And you've done the CDs for me and a lot of other things. I didn't even know how to send a text before you showed me.

I'm glad I've been useful.
As I've said to you before, I've always thought of you, really, as the son I never had, because you're such a nice person.

That's kind of you to say.
Well, it's true. The things you've done for me, you know? You've been fantastic, really. If you stopped coming tomorrow, I would be very upset. It's not only the things you've done but it's the fact you're very giving, very kind

242

person as well, which I like, you know? That's what it boils down to, really.

I haven't really done that much, Kevin.
Well, you have, you know? It's the best thing that ever happened to me, really. That's what I think, anyway. You're like a substitute for the sons I lost, you know what I mean? They'd be your age, if they were still alive. And I think a lot of you, you know, really a hell of a lot of you. It's not love, but it's not far off that, if you know what I mean?

I do. Thanks Kevin. Anyway, I think I've got enough for the book now.
That's great. Let me know when it's ready.

Will do. Speak to you later.
Keep in touch.

I will. Bye Kevin.
Bye Dan.

Printed in Great Britain
by Amazon